THE RESTING PLACE OF THE MOON

Felicity Heathcote

About the author

Felicity Heathcote, a Dublin-based clinical psychologist, teacher and writer has spent several years in Palestine where she conducted workshops for the UN and other non-governmental groups in Gaza and the West Bank. Born in England, she has also worked in Iran, Japan and the USA. Psychologist to the Irish Olympic team in Barcelona and Sydney, she applies her adapted zen techniques to sport, business, the arts and education. Her publications include *Peak Performance: Zen and the Sporting Zone* (1996) and *The Learning Zone* (2000), both published by Wolfhound Press. Committed to human rights and the dignity of the person, she hopes that the *Resting Place of the Moon* will bring home to readers an understanding of daily life in places where conflict and fear brutalise communities and individuals.

To the people in Palestine and Israel who shared their stories, and to all who have suffered and who continue to suffer in this conflict

The Resting Place of the Moon is a modern quest for truth. Set on Jerusalem's fabled Mount of Olives, it is the story of a conference of all the birds of the air, assembled by the Hoopoe bird. The task given to the birds is to reveal to the world some of the consequences of the violence and injustice besetting all who live today in 'The Holy Land'.

It is a tale of such raw pain and deep hurt that its meaning is perhaps more poignant and its healing power stronger when the words are spoken by birds.

The Hoopoe bird's conference aspires to inform, but also to awaken a sleeping world to the daily lives of a nation of people living under the shadows of military checkpoints and the already notorious 'Separation Wall'. The whole world knows the horror of suicide bombings that bring shame to the voice of freedom. The underlying horrors of injustice so often cited as reasons for terror have seldom impinged on the conscience of the free world. As this tale reveals, such injustices bring shame too on all who believe in human dignity and freedom but who do nothing.

The Resting Place of the Moon

Preface by Jeff Halper
Nobel Peace Prize Nominee, 2006

Felicity Heathcote

The OtherWorld Press

This edition: hardcover
10-digit ISBN 0 9546150 2 6
13-digit ISBN 978 0 9546150 2 4
A CIP catalogue record for this title is available from the British Library

THE OTHERWORLD PRESS
68 Mountjoy Square, Dublin 1 Ireland
email: info@bookconsult.com
info@otherworld.ie

Cover by Andre Devereux
Cover illustrations by Vic Lepejian, Jerusalem
Typeset by Oldtown
Printed and bound in Ireland by Betaprint Ltd

CONTENTS

The author's royalties from the sale of this book
will be donated for the benefit of peace and humanitarian groups
for Palestine and Israel.

Acknowledgments

My appreciation and thanks to the many people who have assisted me in various ways in my research and writing of this book: especially my husband, Niall for all his support; my daughter, Clare Simran, for ensuring I completed the book and for accompanying me around Palestine to hear these stories with me at first hand; Jeff Halper for his Preface; Alice Bach for responding to the text; Professor Don Moore, SJ; Zoughbi Zoughbi; Taisir Abdallah, Al Quds University; all the Brothers at Bethlehem University, especially Br Vincent, former President, and Br. Fergus; Nidal and Adnan of Bethlehem; Rima Tarazi Nasir; Tania Tamari Nasir; Amit Leshem; Nazih and Mary Eldin; Des and Jennifer Sinnamon; Susan Hood; Suha and Yussef Dorkhom; Adnan Abu Al-Shabab; Kian Khatabi; Wail Obeidi; Ezra Nebi and Stephen Heydt who did such excellent work as Director of the UNRWA psycho-social programme in Gaza; to all my friends on The Mount of Olives, Jerusalem; Elizabeth Fuller; Hilda O'Connell; Eric Guiry; Sandra Conway; Mary-Elaine Grant; my colleagues at the American College, especially Ronan Yore; Elizabeth Seigne; Jennifer Evans; Ian Tyndall, Niamh Flynn and John McCarron – for their ideas and support; and my students. And to my African Grey parrot for endless vocal encouragement!

My appreciation to the intellectuals and writers in Palestine and Israel whose work and discussions influenced my ideas especially Mahdi Abdul-Hadi; Uri Avnery; Yitzhak Frankenthal; Angela Godfrey; Amira Hass; Gideon Levy; Dr. Ruhama Marton; Ilan Pappe; Tanya Reinhart.

My thanks also to Andre Devereux for his superb cover design; to Vic Lepejian, the Jerusalem artist for his kind permission to base the design on his wonderful illustrations of the Hoopoe bird and of Jerusalem; to Andrew Holohan for his images of birds which decorate the text; to Seamus Cashman, formerly my publisher at Wolfhound Press and now at The OtherWorld Press, for believing in the work, for his detailed editorial assistance, and for publishing this book.

Finally, my thanks to all who purchase this book and thereby contribute to peace and humanitarian groups responding to the Palestine / Israel conflict.

PREFACE

I am pleased and honored to have been asked to write this Preface to Felicity Heathcote's beautiful and imaginative book, *The Resting Place of the Moon.* I had gotten to know Felicity during her time in Jerusalem in my capacity as the director of the Israeli Committee Against House Demolitions (ICAHD), an Israeli peace organisation dedicated to ending Israel's policy of demolishing Palestinian homes (14,000 so far since 1967) and, ultimately, the Occupation itself.

Felicity's book is, indeed, imaginative, and that is important. We Israelis, Palestinians and internationals who have worked so hard over the years in the cause of a just peace have found it extremely difficult to get our analyses, as well as our experiences with Israel's terrible Occupation, across to both the wider public and to decision-makers. We have tried novels, films, lectures, protest demonstrations, lobbying, academic articles and books, conferences, art shows, concerts, happenings – *anything* to convey the horrors of the Occupation. I don't want to say we've failed but, for some reason we cannot fully fathom, Israel's Occupation exists in a bubble that is almost impossible to penetrate. And so it goes on and on, houses of innocent Palestinian families demolished on almost a daily basis (with, of course, no compensation; after all, it is a get out of our way policy), massive settlements established on Palestinian land, a Wall (!) twice as high and five times longer than the Berlin Wall erected which imprisons an entire people, induces poverty, unemployment, hopelessness and even starvation, explicit components of state policy – and all supported by the governments of the world. *Any* new,

7

imaginative attempt to get the message out, to reach the wider public, is welcomed, and nothing more so than stories of birds whose songs, wings and hopefully messages soar, as Felicity writes, above the walls and suffering that, apparently, block our ability to communicate. Her book dares to do what, for some reason, has been deemed undo-able: speak of the troubles of the down-trodden; lay the blame precisely where it belongs, at the doorstep of the oppressor. The cold fact that Israelis – my people, *Jews* for the most part – are the oppressors in this case saddens and mortifies me. But it's true. The birds have told the truth.

Felicity's story is also one of a concerned person moved deeply by the suffering she has witnessed. This is also important, for it is only when we, the people, begin to speak up – or in Felicity's case – *sing out*, will we be able to connect to our fellow global citizens. Governments will not do the right thing unless prodded by us. But most people are not academics or Middle East experts; they do not feel entitled to raise their voices in opposition to all those authoritative prime ministers and generals who seem to tell us 'like it is'. *The Resting Place of the Moon* by-passes all that. It wells up from, and connects to, the primal urge in all of us to do good, to be good, and thus, perhaps, to advocate for the good in terms of pressuring our governments to end the Occupation now, before one more person dies, before one more house is demolished, before the Holy Land becomes so barren from the bulldozers and tanks of the military that, alas, there are no more branches upon which birds can perch and hold their consultations. Literally. Since 1967 Israel has uprooted or cut down *more than one million Palestinian olive and fruit trees*.

As Felicity writes: "The task that Hoopoe gave to the birds of the air in Israel and Palestine is done. They braved the heat and the freezing cold; they flew over burning sands and icy mountaintops; they told their stories…. The task has been passed on to those of us who care, and who know of the story." Let us not ignore the conference of the birds. They have held their counsel and Felicity has made their words soar. Let us take hope in her story and, more so, take up the challenge of the Hoopoe.

The task has passed to us. As we approach forty years of Occupation, two generations of Palestinians who have known no freedom for a minute of their lives (themselves children of refugees from Israel in 1948), let us vow: justice and peace in Jerusalem *this year*!

Thank you, Hoopoe. Thank you, Felicity.

In Peace,

Jeff Halper
Jerusalem, November 2006

Jeff Halper is an Israeli Professor of Anthropology and the Coordinator of the Israeli Committee Against House Demolitions (ICAHD), a non-violent, direct-action Israeli peace and human rights organisation that resists the Israeli Occupation and advocates for a just and sustainable peace. His academic research has focused on the history of Jerusalem in the modern era He has taught at universities in Israel, the US, Latin America and Africa, taking leave of Ben Gurion University to take up the directorship of ICAHD. He works closely with NGOs, diplomats, journalists and activists abroad. He is the author of Obstacles to Peace, a resource manual of articles and maps on the Israeli/Palestinian conflict, published by ICAHD. His new book, An Israeli in Palestine, on his work against the Occupation, will be published soon by Pluto Press.

One winter evening I was walking quietly
along the beach as the pewter light of the full
moon stained the glittering bay. A cry pierced the
still night air and I looked up to see a lone white
seagull glowing translucent in the pale moonlight.

For several minutes the gull hovered motionless
above my head, then gracefully glided out to sea.
When I looked down, I saw a scroll
lying at my feet.

Here is the text that was written on that scroll:
it is the tale of a thousand birds
– a story that has to be told.

Chapter I

JERUSALEM, THE HOLY CITY

*"O Attar! You have scattered on the world
the contents of the vessel of the musk of secrets."*
Mantiq Ut-Tair

The Wall

The magnificent crest of the Hoopoe bird cast a dark shadow over the sandy, green-spiked hills surrounding Jerusalem. Like a crown, her feathered crest formed a proud silhouette against the gilded dawn sky over the eternal city. Her distinctive cry rang out and echoed across the silent valleys and an answering symphony of silver notes and golden chords rose to a heavenly crescendo. As the rhythm of beating wings blended with the murmurings of the cool morning breeze, a group of birds swooped down onto the grey concrete wall and gathered round the Hoopoe bird.

In the distance the golden domes of the Haram al-Sharif and the Russian Orthodox church of St Mary Magdalene sparkled among the olive and pine trees while below, in the Kidron Valley, the tombs slept peacefully awaiting Judgement Day. A new day of hope was dawning as slowly the beautiful cascade of notes from the bird chorus died away across the valley.

Silence reigned as creation acknowledged a state of

timeless perfection. For a brief moment the mechanistic modern world bowed its head in submission to the beauty of nature and time stood still. The birds looked around, suddenly self-conscious as they became aware of the powerful message of their birdsong in such a historical setting.

There was, however, a dark side to this haunting beauty and that was the Wall. This Separation Wall was a sign of domination and intimidation, a symbol of lives stifled by fear and aggression. The birds perched, like tiny specks of dust on this huge structure, which dwarfed the houses as it encircled the villages of Abu Dis. The Wall cut through the campus of the University of Al-Quds and divided the holy city of Jerusalem into a patchwork of disconnected neighbourhoods. This was not just a wall, however, it was an ugly barrier, the effects of which were both psychological and physical. It destroyed the dignity of both Palestinians and Israelis and enraged the watching world as it shattered the lives and livelihoods of a distressed nation.

The noisy chattering of the birds ceased as the Hoopoe began to speak: "I am the Hoopoe bird – many centuries ago my ancestor was a messenger of King

Solomon to the Queen of Sheba – and since the onset of the holy Islamic era we have been beloved and protected by the great prophet Mohammed himself.

I have called you here in order to organise a conference – a conference of birds. Nearly a thousand years ago the Persian poet Farid ud-Din Attar wrote an allegorical tale about an assembly of birds. These birds would embark on a journey full of tribulations and peril in order to find their Sacred King – the Simurgh. Today, in the early days of the third millennium, we are here to arrange a new assembly in order to undertake a different journey. This is a journey which we hope will help to bring about peace and justice in this Holy Land. For a long time now we have all witnessed hate and brutality from many sides but since the start of the second *Intifada* the violence is worsening and this vicious cycle must be broken. We have stood quietly by over the ages and watched as human society has made its mistakes. Now we too must take our place in the arena of peace and understanding. Unless a solution to this problem can be found without delay, this country – and the wider region in which it is located – will never be at peace with itself."

A graceful swallow, Simran, slowly stretched her gleaming neck and asked if she might speak. "You are right, Hoopoe bird, the question of Palestine is at the centre of the crisis in the world and consequently, without an acceptable solution to this grave problem, we cannot have the universal peace we all desire. Why does the world not acknowledge this? Many of the acts of terror committed today throughout the world are carried out by men and women who use the cause of Palestine as a reason or excuse for their violent actions. Surely fewer people would be recruited to carry out such violence if justice were to be brought to bear on the sad situation here?" The other birds muttered their assent softly and with one voice.

Hoopoe went on to explain: "Often the situation in Palestine appears insoluble because it is a story of greed and self-interest – perpetuated first by the colonial powers of bygone days and now replaced by the humiliating tactics used by the occupying forces of today in order to extend their power and control over a repressed people. It is the literal representation of the bible story which states that God gave the Promised Land to the Jewish people and to them alone. It is about a Jewish people who were given a little land to form a nation, which is the right of all nations. They continued, however, to grab more and more from the Palestinian people who failed to establish a state for themselves and consequently lost nearly everything."

"It is a tale of acts of terror, carried out years ago by those Israelis who were then called freedom-fighters, in order to rid this land of British colonialism. Sadly these same acts of terror are repeated today by Palestinians in an attempt to rid their land of Israeli occupation."

"It is a story of a Palestinian people who were intimidated and driven out of their homes and have spent their lives in refugee camps waiting for the right of return to their own land – a right that sadly looks less and less likely to be attained as time goes by."

A slender African Grey parrot, whose name was Einstein, looked on gravely, his dark brown eyes deeply troubled. "Most of the homes are no more," he said sadly. "They have been destroyed and Israeli towns have been built over them. All the birds talk of this. There is often no trace of these Arab villages; even the names have been changed. How can the refugees return, bearing keys for homes and villages that no longer exist?" Einstein began to tug at his feathers. Whenever he was anxious. He would always pull his feathers out one by one, a nervous habit which often resulted in a little bald patch on his wing.

The cry of the *muezzin* rang out from the nearby mosque – "Allah-o-Akbar" – as the Hoopoe continued: "You are right, wise bird, even the rest of the land is now crowded, dotted with illegal settlements. How can refugees now return to an occupied homeland? As scholars have explained, the myth the world perpetuates is that the Palestinians left their homes of their own free will, leaving an inhospitable, barren land. The truth is they left their homes in fear of their lives expecting to return within days. Consequently there was no willing exit from Palestine and their keys remain with them in the refugee camps, after all these years, ready for the day when they can return. The myth the world lives with is that the Israelis moved into abandoned homes and uninhabited land."

Hoopoe paused: "This story has now become the tale of an occupying country supported by the collective guilt of the world and by the single superpower whose politicians allow Israel's might to be perpetuated in this, our Holy Land."

The beautiful song of the nightingale then followed and echoed all their thoughts as he asked: "What can we do? We are only birds; like many humans, we too feel hopeless in this situation. I am named after Hafez, one of the greatest of the Sufi poets who was born centuries ago in Shiraz, the ancient Persian city of nightingales and roses. This Holy Land too is a wonderful place of landscapes filled with lovely birds and flowers. We should make it a place of harmony and peace, not betrayal and distrust. What has gone wrong and how can we birds help to redress the evils we see all around us?"

A tiny sparrow rose on her delicate feet. "My name is Suha and this morning I flew from Bethlehem, a beautiful old town of stately buildings, faded, rose-pink stone against an timeless sky. I came from the gardens of the university overlooking the town and as I gazed across the hills I could see no space for the promised Palestinian state. The countryside is taken up by settlements built on the lands of the local people. These settlements contain many people brought from foreign places, seduced by stories of a land flowing with milk and honey. This, however, is not their land, sadly it is occupied territory. Strengthened by the backing of other nations, they exploit the water resources, which are the life-blood of the local Palestinian villages and they raise up mighty cities full of modern buildings, out of place in this ancient land. Roads leading to villages are blocked off with huge concrete boulders and new bypass roads are being built, for the sole use of the new settlers."

Suha continued to speak, her tiny head shaking from side to side as she emphasised her points with great passion. "Bethlehem has already suffered greatly and soon the apartheid Wall will encircle the town, its people cruelly imprisoned in the very place where Christ was born. Even now it is difficult to leave the town, the people waiting for hours on end at the Gilo checkpoint, just to travel the few miles into Jerusalem, facing humiliation at every turn. Soldiers once again cast their shadow over Bethlehem as Roman soldiers did in ancient times, thousands of years ago when Herod and his descendants ruled the land. Some now, as then, distressed by the brutality around them, have become conscripts in a drama of which they feel no part. Others, to their shame, feel empowered rather than diminished by their acts of violence, both psychological and physical. As we watch these daily occurrences of inhumanity, we are overcome with feelings of helplessness. What can we do to stop this behaviour that affects both the victim and the perpetrator? Sadly, the individual who brutalises also becomes a victim of his own brutality."

Abruptly, Suha the tiny sparrow stopped, afraid that she might have spoken too much.

Again Hoopoe spoke: "You may only be birds but you have within you the wisdom of the ages, beloved by God you fly with the wind and soar to the stars. That is the reason I have called you together, to try to find some solution to this great dilemma which confronts us."

Suddenly what seemed like sparks of fire-light seemed to hurtle past the birds and land with squeaks and squawks in the middle of an old olive tree growing at the base of the wall. Startled, the birds peered down to see a tiny, brightly coloured parrot fluffing out his feathers as he carefully plucked out dried leaves and tiny twigs. Looking up he saw the other birds and acknowledged them with an exaggerated bow. He then rather gingerly made his way to the top of the wall. Shaking himself again, he began to speak:

"Manga the parrot, reporting from Ramallah. I apologise for my delayed arrival but I have flown for several hours over hills and vales. I may not be very strong and I may be very young but I really want to help in any way I can."

Hoopoe stifled a smile as she welcomed the youthful parrot. His enthusiasm was infectious and seemed already to be making an impact on the rest of the group of birds; he was certainly well named, she thought. His feathers were orange and gold, overlapping with bursts of green and bright red, his tiny wings fringed with olive green. Slender strands of lime-green spread out from the scarlet smudges around his eyes, radiating along the top of his small head. Indeed, he looked just like an over-ripe mango.

"Well, Manga, we are in the process of explaining that very few people really know what is happening here. The world only sees one side of this sad and confusing story. It identifies, quite rightly, with the suffering and sadness of the Israelis as they face horrific violence. It grows cold with fear when it confronts views of Palestinians shouting for violence and revenge in Gaza, Nablus and Jenin. This is, of course, one part of the picture: this violence obviously is wrong and has to be condemned. However, what is not portrayed to the world is the daily humiliation and unbearable hardships of the Palestinian people in their own land, all of this harsh treatment being excused on the grounds of security requirements. The killing of babies and young children, however, can never be excused on the pretext of security – or for any other reason. It is not excusable to shoot young children throwing stones at tanks because the soldiers inside are angry or upset. Old men and women should not be insulted or beaten and kept standing in the heat or freezing cold at checkpoints in their own country. Are all these people really security risks? Patients cannot get to hospital and often bleed to death at these checkpoints, while women give birth to dead babies. Is this fair and just behaviour?"

Hoopoe realised that the birds were getting restless, unable to comprehend the severity of the situation and decided to involve them again in a more practical way. "One of the difficulties which we have to face is the question of the very structure on which we are now sitting – the Wall. Another area about which most of the world remains ignorant is the question of the settlements. Built on Palestinian land, these settlements are illegal. The world is repeatedly told that they are being dismantled but in fact, new ones are continually being built and existing ones extended. Every year many more Jewish people are encouraged to come from abroad to join these settlements There is a great deception being perpetrated about both of these subjects. Many promises have been made to the world but few are being kept."

The birds looked around, curiously examining the solidly ugly grey concrete structure on which they were sitting, watching it snake across the countryside, a symbol of oppression and hopelessness. Village cut off from village, family separated from family; for many, the only exit a single locked gate, rarely opened except in the morning and at night.

"The Wall is not a fence which can be dismantled at any moment," Hoopoe continued, "much of it is a massive eight metre high structure, on part of which we are now perched, like specks of dust. Some towns are completely walled in like prisons, with only one locked gate for those who want to enter and those who wish to leave. These people are prisoners in their own homes, like birds in a cage, the sun and sky cut off by this towering structure. The gate is unlocked twice or three times a day at the whim of the soldiers. If they are locked outside their village at the wrong time, they must wait there in extreme cold or heat until the soldiers deem it appropriate to open the gate again. In most of these villages, the crops are outside the Wall and the farmers have great difficulty harvesting his fruit and vegetables. In some places, like the pretty village of Jayyous, many farmers are leaving their fruit to rot, their livelihoods destroyed. Some of the Palestinians' land has been taken because the Wall runs well inside the Armistice line that was agreed nearly sixty years ago as the internationally recognised boundary between the two sides. This Wall has already been deemed illegal by the International Court of Justice in The Hague – but it continues to be built. The land is beginning to resemble a jigsaw puzzle, a jagged line cutting off Palestinian villages from each other and splitting the country into pieces, with no room any more to establish a viable Palestinian state."

A wise old owl, Simsim, spoke out in horror: "Now at last I understand that the Palestinians are living imprisoned like our own dear bird friends in tiny cages, not able to cultivate their own land, to harvest their own crops or to experience freedom which is the right of all peoples. How can they survive? Do they die of sadness as do so many of our captive birds?"

The other birds muttered softly amongst themselves, the full horror of the situation beginning to strike them as they pondered the analogy of captive birds in a cage. Hoopoe bird watched the assembled birds as they reflected on the problems of Palestine. Gently she spoke again: "Many do suffer from psychological disorders and depression, brought about by sadness and a sense of loss, others are blinded or killed and maimed by the fire of guns and missiles. We must remember this happens too in the case of many innocent Israelis. There is terrible suffering on both sides. If we do not acknowledge this fact, peace will never be achieved because only by seeing all points of view do we gain true peace and reconciliation. When we are compassionate, we can understand how other individuals feel; maybe the thought of a bird being kept imprisoned in a cage helps us to understand, just a little, the severity of this problem."

"We are finally beginning to understand the problems of this land", said Simsim, "but what can we do to find a solution?"

"Well," replied Hoopoe, "eight hundred years ago in the ancient land of Persia, the Sufi philosopher Attar wrote a poem about a meeting of many birds who decided to set out on a journey to find the Simurgh, the King of the Birds. Centuries ago, all our ancestors gathered at that famous conference of the birds and now, at the start of a new millennium, we too must come together to undertake a special journey – both physical and metaphysical. As our ancestors watch over us, it is our task to encourage peaceful negotiations and a rejection of the blind alley that is violence. It is also our task to tell the fair and balanced truth and to awaken the sleeping world to the injustice that is occurring in the land of Palestine."

Chapter 2

JOURNEY THROUGH
THE VALLEY OF THE MIND

*"Jewish Mystics tread the earth lightly. Steeped in the
immediacy of the moment, witness to the blessings of
birdsong and bread, they embody their wisdom and
teach by the way they live."*
Pearl Besserman

The birds looked at each other warily, wondering what
exactly Hoopoe bird meant by these strange words.
Once again Hoopoe began to speak.

"The famous philosopher, Attar, tells the tale of
how thousands of birds set off on a journey over high
rocky mountains, through deep, treacherous valleys
and across stormy seas. Scorched by the burning rays
of the sun and frozen by storms of snow and ice, they
battled the forces of nature.

Many birds faced much danger and suffering, as
overcome with the desire to attain understanding of
existence and achieve unity with the Simurgh, the
Sacred King of the Birds, they undertook the perilous
journey. This was a journey from which no bird had
ever returned. Indeed, many thousands of birds died
on the way and only thirty finally reached the palace
of the Simurgh. There, they became one with the
Simurgh, lost in love and harmony as thirty birds

contemplated themselves in a state of true Understanding." The birds were fascinated by this ancient tale and, for once, total silence embraced them as Hoopoe finished her speech. The sound of a cock crowing in the nearby village broke their reverie. "Tell us more about this journey," said Einstein the parrot, holding his grey head on one side, his bright, brown eyes shining as he listened intently.

"It was a journey full of great hardships," responded Hoopoe, "the birds had to traverse seven valleys before they overcame their state of separation and achieved unity with the Simurgh. It was a journey full of anxiety and confusion as difficulties continuously overtook them."

"Is life itself not filled with difficulties?" asked Nasrallah, the proud partridge, as he gently ruffled his brown, multi-speckled feathers.

"Indeed," replied Hoopoe, "the original story of the conference of the birds, so many years ago, is an allegorical tale of a journey through life. This is a journey filled with many troubles and anxieties which end when unity with God is ultimately achieved.

The first valley that the birds had to cross was the valley of the Quest. This was a place of many difficulties, which together conspired to bring about a state of discouragement and despair. When the birds entered this valley they were consumed by the desire to attain that which they sought for so long. Consequently, they had no fear of future tribulations and were driven on by the compulsion to continue their quest. We too must set off on our journey of truth and integrity in this state of mind."

Benjamin, the quail, lowered his head humbly. "I'm not sure I have the courage to undertake such a journey," he said softly.

"We can undertake such a journey if we desire the outcome sufficiently." said Hoopoe kindly, "That is the most important factor. In life, all things are possible."

"The second valley was the valley of Love," continued Hoopoe. "Here love is supreme. In the presence of love, nothing else exists; only the beloved matters – reason has no place. Life without the loved one has little meaning. When love is central to our life, nothing is impossible: everything can be borne for the sake of the beloved. Just as the Sufi poems related so many years ago, the nightingale desires only to be united with its beloved rose – in order to do this, however, it must experience pain, the pain of the thorn. Yet such is the yearning of the nightingale that nothing is feared."

Hoopoe bird paused, "We too must undertake a journey which is carried out with a passionate love of truth and justice." In the distance, the burnished gold of the great Dome on the Rock burst into light, touched by the glowing rays of the early morning sun. Hoopoe hesitated, blinded for an instant by the beauty of the city. Composing herself, she sighed softly and continued:

"After this the birds had to face the third valley of Understanding. This is not the transience of earthly knowledge but the depth of understanding where everything is seen in its true light. When veils are removed from our eyes we see the essence of Being. This knowledge is not gained from books or learning. This does not come from the comforts of life. Understanding emerges from suffering and experience, from empathy and compassion, from reverence and respect, from revelation and forgiveness. When we listen to individual stories of life in Palestine we too will understand what must be undertaken."

Pausing slightly, Hoopoe looked around and saw she was again losing the attention of some of the younger sparrows who were chattering among themselves and joking with Manga, whose easy manner and quick wit had soon made him a favourite. "If you cannot bear with me for a short time, how can you undertake this mammoth task?" she asked sadly. The young birds looked ashamed and settled down again.

Hoopoe bird cleared her throat: "The fourth valley of Independence and Detachment was the next region to be traversed. By this time many birds had given up their journey or had died from exhaustion. The ones that survived learnt the rule of detachment. In this valley, they came to know that they were no longer dependent on anything or anyone, that they had no need to dominate or to possess. It became clear to them that nothing external had any real value as they themselves, became more and more detached from worldly values and material objects. Only an inner state of quiet and stillness was important to them. In this state, the self became lost and was replaced by emptiness. This was not a negative condition but on the contrary it was very positive. After all, it is only by emptying the self that one can become whole."

The birds looked confused by this latest message; they found it difficult to understand the symbolism of those strange words. They were unsure of this paradoxical concept of emptiness, a theme running throughout Christian mysticism, Sufism and Buddhist philosophy.

Einstein, the African Grey parrot, scratched his head in bewilderment. He puffed out his feathers, a scalloped pattern of soft hues of grey, and shook his bright red tail vigorously. "I am the most intelligent and talented of birds," he said. "I can talk all the languages of the human race and I am the greatest mimic of all birds, yet even I do not completely understand what you say, oh wise Teacher."

A young sparrow, Dena, giggled: "You may be the most intelligent but you are certainly not the most modest of birds," she remarked loudly to the delight of the other young sparrows who ruffled their feathers, convulsed with laughter.

Hoopoe continued speaking, frowning at the noisy sparrows as she did so. "If you try too hard to understand my words, you will not succeed. Listen only to your inner voice as pure rational thought will fail you at this time. One of the great psychotherapists of our modern world, Victor Frankl, taught us this. He spent many years in a Nazi concentration camp, a victim of what was probably the greatest crime against humanity of all time. He turned his terrible experiences into something from which he and others could learn and he helped to give a new interpretation to the meaning of existence. He taught us that if we look too hard for happiness, we shall not find it. Therefore, in the same way, you must all stop trying too hard to understand the precise meaning of my words. Just stop and listen to the sublime message contained in the ancient tale of Attar."

The listening birds tried to heed the advice of Hoopoe as she continued: "The birds at this stage progressed to the fifth valley of Unity. In our own fragile world, everything in life is fragmented and there is a great sense of disharmony. When the birds reached this valley, however, they entered a state of unity where there is no separation – everything was as one. The universe may be seen as a sea where each wave is a separate entity rising briefly and then quickly returning to the whole. In the same way, each individual life emerges for a brief span of time and then disappears, returning back to the eternity of universal existence. It is this life of separation that we find painful. Aloneness is not a natural state; before birth and again after death we are one with the universe. Today we must remember that all things on this earth – animals and humans are part of the same universe. We should try to treat everyone with openness and with the same respect we reserve for those who share our views."

By now Abu Dis was awakening, women in *hijab*, wearing long traditional coats with their heads hidden beneath large shawls, were bringing back fresh flat unleavened bread for breakfast. Men were setting out for work in the fields, the chequered grey and white keffiyeh on their heads. For those who had to work in Jerusalem, there was the long trek around to the Jericho road in order to circumvent the Wall. The everyday scene appeared peaceful and normal but beneath the surface was the tension and sadness of life lived under the shadow of the huge Separation Wall.

Hoopoe bird raised her beak and uttered her beautiful cry to regain the attention of the birds. "The sixth valley was the valley of Astonishment and Bewilderment. After the intensity of their attainment of unity the birds were at this point overcome with sadness. Confusion reigned everywhere as the birds tried to come to terms with their latest experiences. We too, in our present task may often be overcome by the enormity of the quest we are undertaking. Confused and distressed we may wish to abandon our endeavour. We must, however, continue with our task until the end."

The more Hoopoe referred to the task before them, the more nervous the birds became. The sufi story now was coming to a close. "Finally the last valley in this mystical quest was reached, the valley of Deprivation and of Death. At last, the meaning of existence could be understood as the birds attained unity with the Sacred One. At this point, consumed by the Divine Beloved, like the moth consumed by the desired flame of the candle, all beings return to dust, taking the entirety of their knowledge with them. We too, dear birds of the sea and of the air, must fulfil whatever destiny God has is in store for us and go on to overcome our fear of death."

A large white seagull, Omar, broke the silence which ensued. "Did the birds really find the Simurgh?" he asked.

"Bird of the sea," answered Hoopoe, "many died on the journey but thirty birds reached the Simurgh and were consumed by their love. Many centuries ago, this story was related by Attar. We now must hold a second conference of the birds in honour of our ancestors; but this time we must bring tales from all over the Holy Land in which we live so that the world may know the truth of what is really happening here."

Taisir, the soft-voiced Jerusalem dove, his beige-pink breast glowing in the clear light, spoke gently: "The Israelis say the Wall is to stop the men of terror from killing innocent people. Is that not a valid reason to divide the country and its warring peoples?"

Hoopoe bird looked kindly at the dove. "You are indeed a bird of peace, an intellectual, who has tried to see this problem from all the different points of view – but sadly this Wall is not just about security against terror," she said. "This Wall will cause much suffering so that rather than becoming a deterrent against evil, it will lead only to more hate and a greater sense of loss. Ultimately, it will be the cause of even more terror. We should have learnt this lesson from the experiences of other countries around the world as should the Jewish people who suffered so much: injustice never stops terror and brutality never stops violence. Dialogue is the important factor; individuals must learn to empathise and talk to each other. Eventually every freedom-seeking group and every government must learn that fact. We ourselves must be a starting point for this worldwide dialogue."

"How can we do that?" asked Benjamin the quail, suddenly fearful of the enormity of the task ahead.

"We shall hold a second conference of the birds on the Mount of Olives," replied Hoopoe. "All birds should set off across this Holy Land and bring back their stories. That is the task you must undertake for the sake of those who are suffering and those who have lost so much."

The birds started to talk together excitedly, at last coming to a realisation of what they were being asked to do. "What kind of stories?" asked Suha the sparrow quietly, a little frightened as she tried to contemplate the importance of the journey awaiting her.

"These must be tales told from all points of view," explained Hoopoe. "There are many stories to tell. There are stories of fear, there are tales of inspiration; there are stories of good and stories of evil. It is our task now to travel throughout the Holy Land to bring back these tales. In several months time we will meet together to hear these stories and decide how to tell a sleeping world what is really happening in our land."

The silver moon was glowing now in the darkening sky and the birds began to prepare themselves to fly away, eager to begin their task. In the breast of each bird were many conflicting emotions. There were feelings of fear and joy, feelings of trepidation and anticipation, but most of all there were feelings of wonder and excitement. They were beginning to realise that, although they were only birds, they too could make a difference to the world. Maybe they could teach others what they had just learnt – that it is indeed possible to make a difference in life; and that to make such a difference it is necessary to understand that every journey must begin with just one single step.

Chapter 3

THE CONFERENCE DAWNS

"If you succeed through violence at the expense of
others' rights and welfare, you have not solved the problem,
but only created the seeds for another."
The Dalai Lama

The Mount of Olives

The day of the conference of the birds had finally arrived. Birds were gathered along the entire crest of the Mount of Olives, on the branches of gnarled olive trees and scented pines, peeping shyly out of tall Cypress trees or perched on low walls bordering the winding stony paths. Thousands of birds were there, each one with its own special story. All of them felt it was a matter of great pride and honour to follow in the spiritual path trodden many centuries earlier by the famed Sufi poet, Farid ud-Din Attar. The birds were also very aware that they were spread right across the fabled hill, where two thousand years earlier Jesus Christ himself had walked.

The morning air was cool as the scent of wild rosemary perfumed the breeze. At the base of the Mount of Olives, many of the birds were resting in the Garden of Gethsemane, where Christ had spent the last night praying in anticipation of his death. Here some of the most ancient olive trees in the whole land could be found, their twisted branches bowed down, weary with the memories of the centuries.

Hoopoe bird stepped forward to welcome everyone to the conference: "Just as eight hundred years ago our ancestors came together to search for enlightenment and joy in the attainment of unity with the King of the Birds, so today we all meet together in a search for peace and justice in this Holy Land. Many years ago my ancestor was the messenger of the wise King Solomon who alone among men spoke the language of the birds. This sacred messenger bird brought back stories from other countries, information the king's army could utilise for battles. This proud bird was also the means by which the mighty nation of the Queen of Sheba was guided to Allah, the Great the Merciful, away from the worship of the Sun God.

It is our task, today, to follow in the path of our ancestors and to soar on wings of eagles in order to bring knowledge and understanding to the world. There are so many stories of suffering of both Palestinians and Israelis," Hoopoe said sadly, "so many that not even the thousands of birds who are here now can relate all of them. In this as in everything, however, we must start with one small step. I shall now take that first step with a moving tale from Bethlehem, the birthplace of Christ."

The City of David

"I am not sure if it is my destiny to write books during difficult times. But writing in such a context becomes an act of non-violent resistance: resisting being silenced, resisting being a spectator, and resisting giving up." Mitri Raheb

Standing on the twisted branch of an old olive tree, Hoopoe surveyed with pride the multi-coloured carpet of birds spread before her. In a strong, clear voice she started with her story:

— Every year, people all around the world celebrate the birth of Christ on Christmas Day. For two thousand years, stories have been told of the shepherds watching their flocks in the field and of wise men seeing a star which guided them to the cave in Bethlehem. Now this historic place is no longer a place of beauty but a sad town, a place of harassment, guarded by checkpoints, surrounded by settlements and cut off by a monstrous Wall. During the curfews imposed on Bethlehem the children were not allowed to go to school, the university was closed and businesses were shut down. This was a particular problem during the thirty-nine day siege, when the Church of the Nativity was besieged causing great social and economic hardship in the small town. —

Suha nodded her head in agreement as she remembered those terrible days. "It was such a difficult time. Children were terrified as the missile bombardment continued day and night. One young child had been confined under curfew for a whole week in her home. When she looked out of her window she saw huge tanks and talked wistfully of being a bird and flying away to freedom. These children have had no childhood."

Hoopoe nodded in assent: "Many many children experience great difficulties as a result of years of Israeli bombing. Some children suffer so much trauma that they are unable to speak for many years, others are very aggressive or anxious or unable to concentrate at school. There are many wonderful people working with such children in Bethlehem and elsewhere."

"It is not only children who are affected," added Einstein. "One story involving an adult during the siege of the Church of the Nativity is particularly distressing, One day during the siege of the church, the old Armenian bell-ringer, Samir, was shot dead by an Israeli sniper just because he wanted to ring the church bells. He was a simple man who did not understand what was going on. He did what he was supposed to do and died because of it."

"That was a tragic case," agreed Hoopoe bird, "and many people have died in that way. Now we shall all begin to read and tell our tales in the words of the humans. I am going to start with an inspiring story about a family who were able to stand up to the military."

Hoopoe shook her crested head and composing herself she began to speak:

— One day many soldiers went to the house of Maher, an eight-year-old boy, on the pretext of searching for weapons. Maher in a very gentle way told the soldiers to come in because the family had nothing to hide. 'Shut up,' the Israeli captain replied harshly and ordered everyone to 'Sit down, don't move, don't look at us, look down. If not, something unpleasant is going to happen to you.'

Maher rushed to his father in tears and asked his parents 'Didn't you teach us to love our enemies, didn't you instruct us to be nice to everyone?' One soldier moved and pointed the gun towards the parents. Adel, the six-year old boy, screamed: 'You dare not shoot at my parents – they are friends of the world!' — At this point Hoopoe paused. The listening birds were all amazed by the reaction of this small child.

"That was so brave," sighed Manga, full of admiration for the child.

Hoopoe smiled, "Young children and young birds speak from the heart, they are not aware of the dangers that may befall them." She continued on with her story.

— The father hugged his oldest son Maher, telling the captain and his soldiers. 'I would like to reaffirm my son's invitation to you, that you are welcome but not in uniform and without your weapons. You are welcome as human beings but definitely not as the apparatus of an evil occupation. You are welcome as human beings who respect us, not as individuals embodying torture, maiming or instilling fear in our children.'

The Israeli captain replied sarcastically: 'Stop terrorism and you will have a better life.' The mother, Elaine, replied, 'All kinds of violence should be stopped including state violence. It is illegal, get out of the territories, then you will see a different relationship.' —

The birds held their breath at these words, apart from Einstein who decided to support the mother's brave words. "It is so sad, how the world is prepared to accept violence and abuse when it is the agents of a state that are the perpetrators."

— Ahlam, the twelve-year old girl, echoed her mother's point of view. 'If you leave us alone we will not be subjugated to violence and we will not use it. Your guns make us scared, we want to live our own childhood, we want to play, we want to have fun, we are tired of seeing blood.' —

The birds murmured in agreement. "There are many people in Bethlehem and the West Bank who have never left their home town and have never seen the sea," said Jacob, a small owl. "They are forbidden to leave because they have West Bank identity cards. Israeli children can play in parks and swim in the sea but Palestinian children are prisoners in their own land, many surrounded by a Wall."

— The father noted: 'Our children are not able to enjoy nature, summer or spring. We enjoy seeing the red in roses and not in the spilling of our blood. Get out as an occupier and you will be welcome as a friend. We would like to give our children hope that life does not equal death. Let us all celebrate life and appreciate differences. Let us see justice and deepen the roots of humanity.'

"That is true," said another sparrow, "and that we must always acknowledge but I have yet another brutal tale coming from Bethlehem checkpoint. Gideon began to tell his tale:

— "Bethlehem University is a very special Institution which provides the young people of Palestine, both Christians and Muslims with an excellent education. This gives them the opportunity of self-discovery through learning and the tools for creative life-building through knowledge. This education also helps to strengthen the students intellectually, morally and spiritually so that they may be peacemakers of the world."

Einstein nodded enthusiastically, "Indeed this university has a wonderful reputation and functions under very difficult circumstances. These have included long periods of curfew and military attacks during the first few years of the *Intifada* when every building on campus was damaged."

Gideon continued with his sad story. "One day a young student was taken seriously ill and needed immediate treatment in Hadasseh, an Israeli hospital, where he had been two days earlier with heart problems. When he reached the checkpoint, the soldiers refused to let the ambulance go through. His parents then went through all sorts of channels attempting to get him to the Israeli hospital which was waiting to receive him. Finally after a long delay at the checkpoint he died. He was just twenty two."

Suha began to speak once more her voice trembling with sadness and anger: "That is a heartbreaking story and as we know, just one of many. How can these people sleep at night? Have they no compassion? Have they no imagination? Can they not visualise their own friends or relatives in the same position?" She stopped to wipe away a tiny tear. "We must not view all soldiers in this light, however; despite these stories, there are soldiers who try to help and others who truly dislike the job they have to carry out."

— One day a nursing co-ordinator in a hospital outreach ambulance was driving with a clinical team through a Bethlehem checkpoint. As usual he showed the soldier his ID card and his permit. The soldier noticed the date of expiration on the permit and started to laugh happily. 'That is a lucky day,' he exclaimed 'That is the day my military service ends. I hate the things this army, this country and this government make us do. I cannot wait to leave this army. Your name Nasrallah means victory, that is good for this country. Now because of this date, I will let all of you through without checking your permits.' —

Suha paused: "Now you can see the dilemma many people are facing in the land of Israel at this time. Is that soldier a traitor?"

Ameer, a white dove, stepped forward, "I think that he is certainly no traitor, rather he is someone who follows his conscience, someone who believes that the policy he is forced to follow is unjust. Many of the Israeli military, those who call themselves the *Refuseniks*, would rather go to prison than serve in the Occupied Territories. Some soldiers try to pretend that they are physically ill or psychologically disturbed, still others choose to go to jail as a matter of conscience. This is not an easy decision and leads to a life of isolation and disgrace but it is maybe preferable to living with the shame of abusing, both physically and psychologically, Palestinian civilians in their own land."

"Are these soldiers unpatriotic?" asked Rebecca, the quiet peacock.

"No," replied Suha, "they care very much about their country but they realise that violence is not only ineffective, it is also counterproductive. The brutal actions of soldiers produce a spiral of violence that perpetuates the problem. It is not easy for soldiers to break their silence. The soldiers who go to prison are true patriots but they suffer because armies do not want solders to think. Sadly, it is also true that most governments do not like their citizens to reflect and criticise events in their own land."

A large sparrow called Bassem came up to change places with Suha:

— I am going to tell you about a famous camera man, Khaled from Bethlehem. Over the years he has been a familiar figure, camera in hand, in the occupied territories, as he made documentaries about life in the refugee camps. Khaled explained how 'One night during the siege of Bethlehem a soldier with whom I was friendly suddenly changed his attitude towards me. He told me to go home and he said that the next time he met me he would shoot me. Next day, near Deheisha refugee camp, he saw me and he shot at me, he shot my arm, my leg and my back while I kept filming his actions with my camera. The following day I was back shooting more scenes, the soldier saw me again and grabbed my camera, threw it under his tank and drove over it. Then he shouted at me: 'Why did you throw your camera under my tank?' —

Bassem then explained: "Khaled worked for Bethlehem Television and his documentaries were well known so many people think that the soldiers were trying to intimidate him and stop his excellent work."

The birds were quite shocked and disheartened by the news of all these stories. In the pale blue arched sky, a golden orb hung suspended between heaven and earth. For a few minutes silence reigned as they reflected on the tales they had heard. Then, suddenly, they started to talk animatedly amongst themselves. They were chattering freely about tales of horror and tales of bravery. It was as if a screen had been drawn across an abyss, cloaking their unbearable sadness with serenity and hope.

Chapter 4

LAYERS OF SADNESS

"A point of no return may soon be reached with consequences that may be appalling for Israel and the Palestinians, for the region, and perhaps for the entire world."
Noam Chomsky

Golden rays of sunlight streamed through the interlaced olive boughs as Hoopoe bird stepped forward ready to continue with the stories. In the shade a group of young sparrows were playing a game of oliveball with great glee. Happily they pushed a dusty black olive around the path, skilfully manoeuvring it through two tiny piles of stones. Manga shouted instructions while perched on a bank of scented pine needles, exhorting the birds to follow the rules. "Bassem, do not touch the olive with your claw, only with your beak." At this the sparrows started to argue among themselves. Bassem began to sulk and turned his back on the rest of the sparrows. Suha ignored him and prodded the olive back into position. The game continued and Manga lay back, blissfully closing his eyes as he idly pecked at a rosehip.

Hoopoe watched the proceedings with amusement for a while and then again uttered her distinctive cry in order to gain the attention of the group of birds. Her pale cinnamon crest, tipped with black and white, fanned out as she began to speak: "We have heard some of the trials and tribulations suffered by the people of Bethlehem, now we must move on to other parts of this tragic land. Our friends the quails will tell us tales from Jayyous in the northern West Bank. They will tell us how their once wealthy and vibrant townland is being strangled by this wire-mesh fence and concrete Wall."

The Village of Olive Groves

"Between mute submission and blind hate – I choose the third way. I am samid (passive resistance)." Raja Shehada

The old quail stepped forward with his story from Jayyous. Other birds moved aside as he made his way carefully to the front.

"My name is Ali. I come from the town of Jayyous, once a thriving town full of industrious people, proud of their town, their crops and their olive groves. I have been given this petition by the mayor of Jayyous. He wants the world to know what is happening to his once proud town."

Ali cleared his throat and began to read the petition, slowly and carefully:

'We, the People of Jayyous, respectfully request your presence to witness the damaging environmental, social and economical effects of the Israeli Separation Wall on the town of Jayyous. The Separation Wall wriggles and sprawls to swallow much of the land of Jayyous. Its footprint in the town of Jayyous alone will require the destruction of five hundred dunums of our agricultural land. The Wall, built well within the territory of the West Bank, rather than on the internationally recognised 1967 border, will effectively depose nine thousand dunums – two thousand five hundred of which are irrigated croplands.'

"What does that mean?" asked Manga, holding his head on one side as he tried to understand the strange words being read out.

"It is quite simple," said Ali wearily, "it means a loss of land and livelihood. Land which is behind the new Wall – and that is most of the village, can only be reached with great difficulty. There is a law that states that if land is not cared for, it can be confiscated by the Israelis after three years. Consequently, these ancient olive trees which no one can now tend may be lost and the land taken over for new settlements."

Ali wanted to continue; like all the birds he found explanations distressing:

'The seizure will result in the loss of one hundred and twenty green houses, over fifteen thousand olive trees, fifty thousand citrus trees, six out of seven ground water wells (the town's main source of water) and livestock pasture. This land not only supports five hundred and fifty village families but also provides produce to sixty thousand inhabitants of the West Bank.'

Ali stopped reading, his words drowned out by the indignant chatter of the birds rising to a crescendo as they pondered the solemn words of the mayor.

"That is so unjust," cried Simran the swallow, stamping her tiny feet indignantly. "The Palestinians are suffering great deprivation all the time, the Israelis are ruining their livelihood. No one can live without water and the loss of the olive groves is more than just the loss of income, it is the symbolic destruction of hundreds of years of life and culture in the Holy Land. This cannot go on."

Acknowledging the emotional outburst of the young swallow, Ali continued with the statement of the mayor:

'Despite numerous objections, the construction of the Wall has proceeded over the past year, often under the cover of military imposed curfews. The Wall has destroyed and closed six dirt roads and left only one dirt road open as a proposed gate. These measures have hindered the farmers' possibility of reaching their farmlands and of harvesting olive and citrus produce. In order to avoid the transformation of a thriving and self-sustaining community into a refugee camp, the people of Jayyous call upon international opposition to the Israeli Separation Wall. We demand to have free access to reach our land and to keep the rights of ownership to this land.'

The quail stopped speaking. Then bowing low he solemnly concluded: "Thus utter the People of Jayyous in their suffering."

The scribbling of the owls became more furious as they tried desperately to write down all of the information, barely managing to take a break and relax their aching claws before the next bird began to speak.

Jacob, another quail, stepped forth eagerly to speak: "Because of the Separation Wall, Jayyous is no longer a wealthy community. In the local school only nineteen parents of nearly four hundred children have jobs. The other parents are unemployed or farmers with very little income. One quarter of the children cannot afford the very small registration and book fee required by the school each year. This is a direct result of the policy of the Wall."

"This occupation has caused so many problems, financial, historical and emotional." said Maha, a shy quail, emboldened by the stories of the other birds. She continued breathlessly, anxious to contribute to the conference.

— "One day, I saw the usual line of cars queuing up at the Jayyous checkpoint, waiting to return to the town. All over Palestine, people spend hours every day waiting at checkpoints depending on the whim of individual soldiers. At best, it is simply a waste of time and a big drain on both the Palestinian and Israeli economies; at worst, it is a cause of enormous humility and suffering.

On this particular day, people were standing out in the glaring sun and an old man stepped down from an ambulance and explained to anyone who wanted to listen to him his need to reach Nablus everyday to undergo kidney dialysis. 'It's very painful,' he said, pointing to the scars on his arm. 'My son wants to give me one of his kidneys but we would have to go to Jordan for that operation. The Israelis will not let him go because he was once in prison.'

The old man shrugged, resigned to his fate, his eyes filled with pain as he continued his long wait in the mid-day heat." —

Maha was getting angry now, forgetting her shyness and banging the podium with her beak. Einstein watched fascinated, wondering was her beak going to splinter from the ferocity of her attacks on the stones. "I find it so difficult to watch such suffering day by day, year in year out." Said Maha, "The world must stop this injustice."

Simsim, the gentle old owl, looked very sad as he acknowledged the suffering of people throughout the country: "Humiliation and intimidation are major factors at checkpoints. Palestinians cannot travel freely in their own land. Most Palestinians are resigned, however, to this treatment because they feel there is little they can do about their situation. They suffer great anguish in silence."

The rays of the sun were at their hottest now on this warm autumn day but the birds showed no signs of tiring as they stepped forward one by one, eager to tell their stories. The scent of herbs and flower blossoms grew sweeter as the day wore on and the flight of the humming bees slowed as they lumbered heavily from bush to bush. It seemed as if nature itself was suspended in time, lost in the quest for truth and justice for all involved in this enduring conflict.

Next it was the turn of the parrots. All the birds were looking forward to the presentation from Tulkarem by this popular group. Einstein, the intelligent African Grey parrot was well respected and the tiny, brightly-coloured Manga was also regarded by all the birds with great affection.

The Walled City

"We have no known Einsteins, no Chagall, no Freud or Rubinstein to protect us with a legacy of glorious achievements. We have no Holocaust to protect us with the world's compassion."
Edward W. Said

Adjusting his tiny spectacles, Einstein drew a large map in the soil. Using a long twig he pointed out the path of the Wall which encircled the northern towns of Qalqiliya and Tulkarem. The birds tried to see what was happening, crowding forward, craning their necks to see the drawing in the soil. The scribes attempted to copy the map onto their pieces of tree bark. Einstein pointed out that these two important towns are suffering greatly, now virtually cut off from the rest of Palestine. "At some places from the Israeli side the view is merely that of an eight foot wall, soil is banked up and prettily landscaped with trees and bushes to hide the true size of the construction. On the Palestinian side, however, the view is of a twenty-four foot high, ugly, concrete monster creeping across the countryside. Due to the presence of this Wall, the people in these towns undergo great suffering."

Rebecca looked puzzled. "Why do the Israelis try to hide the Wall?" she asked.

"They are afraid of world opinion if the true facts are revealed," answered Suha, the forthright young sparrow, "that is why they talk constantly of the fence, not the Wall."

"Maybe," added Taisir thoughtfully, "If the world knew the full extent of the humiliation that is being perpetrated on the Palestinian people, it would be much more concerned."

"Exactly! Foreigners are discouraged from entering and Israelis are not allowed to enter the West Bank and Gaza – for their own safety. That means that no-one ever sees the true extent of the occupation," said Einstein as he straightened up. "Now let us continue with the story of Tulkarem – so that the world can learn more facts. This also used to be a thriving town, loved by all, a town where everyone lived together in peace. The governor of Tulkarem expressed his sadness at the fate of both Israelis and Palestinians when he said that the Israelis were friends years ago before the start of the first *Intifada*."

Einstein looked around thoughtfully as he continued with another story which confirmed these views.

— One physician who now works in a hospital in Jerusalem, Dr Rami, echoed these sentiments when he said: 'I was a child before the first *Intifada* we used to play football here with the Israeli soldiers.' He pointed to the new concrete checkpoint, which had been a mere field when he was a child, as he described one incident when he and his sister were young children and his father was a doctor working in an Israeli hospital.

'Every Friday we would go to pick apricots and cherries. One day my sister was playing when she dropped an apricot, which rolled into the road. Running after it she was hit by a Palestinian taxi. She flew into the air and fell into the gutter. My father ran to take her to his car but dropped his keys, which he couldn't find. Picking up the bleeding unconscious child he started to wait by the side of the road. The first car to pass was an Israeli police car; they took my father and sister to a hospital. My mother and I stayed on the road very shocked and frightened. A car stopped with an Israeli family inside, my mother spoke to them in Hebrew and they drove us to a nearby Arab-Israeli village. For many years we kept in touch with that family. Now we are afraid of each other.' —

Einstein looked thoughtful again as he carefully preened his dark red tail feathers: "Since the last *Intifada*, many young Palestinian children have never met Israeli children. We need to see all people as human beings not enemies. When we do this we can start to talk and negotiate, that is always the first step." Deep in thought, Einstein stepped down from the podium and perching quietly on one leg stood on an old tree trunk which was covered with green moss.

Another African Grey, Hussein, made his way to the podium. "I can at least bring some good news because great strides are being made on the Palestinian side. There is a group called MEND that follows a path of non-violence. This group was set up by Lucy Nuseibeh, who has been committed to peaceful negotiations for many years." He paused, brushing a feather out of his eyes as he read from a paper held tightly in his sharp claws.

"This organisation established groups all over the West Bank and Jerusalem in order to educate and to help the youth of Palestine to turn away from violence. All sorts of programmes are taught, including sport, drama, art and creative-writing. Children and young people are also helped to deal with stress in a constructive way. It is wonderful to see the way the young people have embraced these ideas. They write and act out plays about violent incidents and learn how to deal with real-life situations of that nature. Furthermore, they are also learning to fulfill their potential and achieve personal excellence in many areas. Developing their talents has come to be seen by them as exciting and they are beginning to view life in a constructive rather than destructive way." Hussein waved his paper enthusiastically in the air: "It is amazing to hear them talking and wonderful to see the change in their thought patterns and in their behaviour. These projects are a wonderful way forward to bring fresh hope to the young people of Palestine."

"But you are right," said Manga, scratching his colourful head as he pondered the dilemma. "How can Israelis be regarded as friends if Palestinians only come into contact with them as soldiers involved in humiliation and harassment at checkpoints; and how can Israelis view Palestinians in a positive light if they associate them only with acts of terror. There are, however, some wonderful Israeli groups that try to arrange for Palestinian and Israeli children to play soccer together. Sport is obviously a great way to unite children of all nationalities and all creeds. These children go away on summer camps sponsored by an Israeli peace centre and learn how to communicate with each other and understand the problems involved in this conflict."

Manga paused for a short time trying to find the right words:

"Einstein talks in more sophisticated language when he says humans need to negotiate but I suppose he really means people of all races have to get to know each other and learn that they are all the same. All people basically want peace and happiness, all people cry, all people bleed and all people ultimately die. The important point is that Palestinians and Israelis must meet together more as human beings."

The birds reflected on this point, as they began to realise how often a culture of violence was based primarily on sheer ignorance of one's opponent.

"Thank you all for your stories. Qalqiliya and Tulkarem are places of great suffering and the world must hear these stories," said Hoopoe thoughtfully as she smoothed down her royal crest. "Now we must hear the stories brought from Ramallah by our friends the pigeons."

The Heights of the Lord

A House
so the olive oil may flow
and candlelight flicker
and between the cracks the soul grows.
Zakaria Mohammed

Manga turned to Hoopoe bird. "The pigeons will now bring stories from Ramallah," he said eagerly, "but firstly I would like to say a few words brought from the Muqata where President Arafat has been confined for nearly three years." Hoopoe smiled and nodded, encouraging Manga to continue. Manga started to speak with great solemnity as he read from a small scroll of paper:

"President Arafat would like the world to know more about the Separation Wall. In particular he wants the world to see the Wall around Bethlehem, the place where Christianity began. Soon the people of Bethlehem will be prisoners in their own town, just as, for the last few years, Yasser Arafat has been a prisoner in his own building, the Muqata. The Israelis refuse to let him leave and conduct the business of running Palestine yet they use his presence as an excuse for the failure of the peace process. This must not continue. I shall now introduce the pigeons of Ramallah to bring forth more stories."

Manga bowed low and stepped down from the podium. A gentle old pigeon Abraham bobbed stiffly up and down as he approached the podium. Putting on his spectacles he continued with the story of Manga.

— "Perhaps President Arafat should have done more to stop the senseless violence perpetrated by some of his followers but it was not easy for him because of the continual Israel provocation. An admission that the violence of the second *Intifada* was clearly counter-productive would probably also have been the right thing for him to do. At that time, however, there were few who could have convinced the majority of Palestinians that they must find other ways to wake up the world and rid their country of Israeli occupation."

Abraham peered short-sightedly over the top of his spectacles as he carried on speaking.

— "Yasser Arafat is a proud man and his people expect him to maintain the right of return for Palestinian refugees who were forced to flee their homeland. Perhaps he should have accepted Israel's limited offer of land as a first step and then demanded more. Despite the mistakes he may have made, however, the main obstacle to peace both now and in the past has been the position of the Israeli government.

How could the Israelis return those large expanses of the West Bank that are already covered in illegal

Jewish settlements? What would be the reaction of the Israeli settlers if they were forced to leave their new homes? Even if there had been sufficient political goodwill, it now seems increasingly less likely that Israel would ever willingly return to its pre-1967 boundaries. All the more reason therefore to find a scapegoat. Maybe that was one of President Arafat's main faults, that he left himself open to being blamed and thereby played straight into Israel's hands." —

"Was he involved in corruption, as people claim?" asked Cyrien.

— "He certainly tried to help everyone who came to him asking for assistance. Maybe some of the people who surrounded him and shielded him from the outside were not the most honest. Was that corruption? All I know is that for the last three years he has personally lived a very simple life. Confined largely to a single conference room in the Muqata and besieged by Israeli forces who destroyed his compound and left gaping holes in the walls of his living quarters, he could hardly be accused of living a life of luxury. Despite these hardships, he has nevertheless remained totally dedicated to the Palestinian cause and appears to maintain an unbroken spirit in a situation that would have defeated a lesser man." —

Hassan, a slender silver grey pigeon stepped forward. "One story he often tells with great glee," he said smiling, "is about the time, many years ago, when he outwitted the Israelis. He went to the house of a friend in Jerusalem and as he arrived he received a message that the Israelis were going to raid the house. He informed his friend of this and begged his friend to leave with him but the friend refused to go. Yasser Arafat then left the house immediately alone. He always recounts with a big smile how thirty minutes after his departure the Israelis arrived and arrested his friend instead of himself."

"Jerusalem is an important issue for him and for all Palestinians," mused Simran the swallow. "It is there, that the Palestinians want to establish their capital when they are finally given a state. The childhood home of Yasser Arafat is in the ground of the Al Aqsa Mosque and eventually he wants to be buried there."

"He is very ill at this very moment in Paris," said Manga sadly, "if he dies, the Israeli government will not allow him to be buried in Jerusalem."

"It is very strange," said Hassan, "the way Israelis can dictate what the Palestinians can and cannot do in their own country."

"Especially as they are the illegal occupiers of our land," added Wail as he made his way to the podium, his feathers gleaming in the sunlight. "I just want to tell people about the eerie silence which settles over Ramallah when they impose a curfew. There is no one in the streets and then the stillness is broken by the ominous rumbling of huge tanks as they patrol the neighbourhoods, crushing cars that get in their way like tiny matchboxes." Wail shook out his dark grey feathers and slowly stepped down from the podium.

Bird after bird told their stories until the dying rays of the sun went down behind the Golden Dome. As the light began to fade, the wild dogs started to howl in the distance and many pairs of inquisitive bright eyes peered out from under the bushes. A group of stray cats were chased away by some of the larger crows; yet, despite the noise, the birds felt strangely at peace. Manga drowsily tucked his head under his wing and balancing on one leg started to sleep, nestling close to Omar, the large seagull. All around them other birds were also sleeping as the Hoopoe bird watched and stood guard, pensively mulling over the activities of the day. Overhead, the hand of Allah spread a midnight-blue veil across the endless sky and a thousand stars were scattered like tiny specks of gold dust across a twinkling velvet backdrop.

Chapter 5

FLIGHTS OF FREEDOM

Blessed are the merciful: they shall have mercy shown them
.Blessed are the peacemakers: they shall be called sons of God.
Matthew 5:1–12. Sermon on the Mount

At sunrise the cocks began to crow and the misty, rose-streaked sky swelled with the sounds of bird song. Drops of dew sparkled like rainbow coloured crystals in the morning sunlight. Tiny blue flowers were scattered over spiky-leafed rosemary bushes and thirsty birds began to drink from delicate, translucent petals. Other birds bathed happily, preening and fluffing out their soft feathers in the warm rays of the sun. Finally refreshed, they all settled down, focussing their attention on the podium.

Hoopoe sat quietly and watched as a tiny spider spun a gossamer web across the small olive branches. As if in a trance, the spider meticulously weaved his fragile path back and forth, moving slowly with the rhythm of time. The spider appeared lost in perfection of action as if he was unaware of which was the spider and which was the web.

Slowly Hoopoe began to speak: "Look at the spider moving backwards and forwards spinning and re-spinning his delicate web. Observe his persistence; see how he never gives up, even when the silken threads break. Watch as he lets go of the self, lost in the task he is performing, neither elated by success nor upset by failure, living always only in the present. We too must behave this way, concentrating on our task, persistent to the very end, mindful only of what we must do. The first day of our conference was a wonderful experience – *Alhamdu lillah!* I am very proud of the way in which you have all presented your stories. We have all learned a great deal about daily events in our beloved country and stories have been told with great passion and dignity. We heard tales of sadness and tales of courage, sources of inspiration for us all. Please continue again today with your moving stories."

One by one the owl chorus made their way to the side of the podium, carefully adjusting their quill pens which hung loosely on twine around their necks and opening up their scrolls.

"Now," said Hoopoe, "we are ready to continue with our tales. The wise owls have unrolled their manuscripts and we will hear stories from Nablus told and read to us by our noble friends, the eagles."

The Well of Jacob

"We, soldiers of the IDF, men and women, hereby declare that we will take no part in the continued oppression of the Palestinian people in the occupied territories, and we will not participate in policing actions or in guarding the settlements."

A sound of the beating of powerful wings filled the air as a beautiful eagle swooped over the upturned heads of the birds and landed gracefully on the stone podium. He began to address the assembly:

"My name is Uri and I am very honoured to be here today at this historic conference. My ancestors have lived in this beautiful land for centuries. Many years ago a medieval philosopher wrote of a Crusader castle high on a hill overlooking the Jordan Valley – 'WHERE EAGLES NEST; THE RESTING PLACE OF THE MOON'. We do indeed nest in the wilderness, on top of lofty mountains and overlooking plains and rivers of great beauty. At night we soar on outspread wings, our companions the translucent moon and shimmering stars."

"Today I have brought tales from the ancient town of Nablus. It is a city surrounded by the beautiful hills of Samaria, a town of great biblical significance, where Jacob built a well on his return from Mesopotamia. Tradition states that at this same well, Jesus asked the woman from Samaria for water. In the old city many minarets of ancient mosques can be seen against the sky-line and people can drink coffee in the old Turkish baths seated on large embroidered cushions. This is also a West Bank town which has long been a place of great suffering."

Uri began his tales:

— Many young boys were sent to prison during the first *Intifada* for throwing stones, some were imprisoned on false charges. One sixteen-year-old boy from Nablus, Mohammed, was imprisoned by the Israelis for two years. At this age he was still regarded as a child. This is a violation of human rights under international law and even under Israeli law. He was not allowed to go to Megiddo prison because he was under age. His best friend, after being badly beaten by Israeli intelligence personnel, had accused him of throwing stones."

Uri began to read aloud from a page of paper he held.

— Mohammed told us: 'They took me away and they didn't tell my mother where I was for two months. My father had died when I was very young, so she was had to bear this alone. I had a beautiful young canary which I used to feed by hand everyday. Shortly after I was imprisoned, my canary died.'

"That is so sad," said Manga, balancing on one leg and spreading out his wing as he tried in vain to hide his tears.

— 'For one month I was tortured,' continued Mohammed, 'and the hand-cuffs were so tight I began to bleed. I would shout a hundred times to go to the bathroom. It was during the first Gulf War and if, when they were questioning me, they heard a bomb alert they would put on their chemical suits and gas masks and then immediately put a pencil between my fingers and squeeze tightly. Then they would push back my head, putting a hand under my chin. I would stop breathing and lose consciousness. At this stage they would stop and throw cold water over me.' —

The birds shuddered at the thought of this brutality especially against a boy who was no more than a child. "How barbaric this behaviour is!" exclaimed Simran indignantly, "This poor child was accused of throwing stones, it is a very minor offence – stones thrown against a huge tank from a long distance."

Taisir looked thoughtful, "Many children have been shot dead for that minor offence."

Uri looked up briefly from the paper he was holding, "Many children have been shot dead for no reasons whatsoever – through the windows of school classrooms, walking in the street, in the arms of their parents," he muttered darkly before returning to the words of Mohammed.

— 'Then I was sent to Naqab prison in the Negev Desert. We stayed in small tents which were unbearably hot in the summer and freezing cold in the winter when the rain and wind tore through them. We were all under enormous stress and had to try to keep ourselves sane by studying, reading and playing table tennis. Some prisoners started shouting and hallucinating. Some turned for support to various political groups in the prison even if they had never been associated with politics before; others started asking for food and still others became depressed. One poor man from Bethlehem went completely crazy; he was shouting all the time. I was depressed but I tried not to show it to the others. We did not eat any meat for two years and on one occasion when we finally did eat meat, I kept the bones as a reminder of that day.'

'In order to stay sane, I tried to plan some goals for the future. My first goal was to finish my school exams or towjihi and then I wanted to go to university to study nursing. For one year there were no visits. Then all of us stopped eating in order to have visits from our families. The prison authorities finally allowed us to have one half hour visit a month, although our families were not allowed to bring anything into the prison for us. For the most part we had to depend on each other for support.' —

Uri stopped reading and, with his head bowed stepped back down from the podium.

A young sparrow, Ahmed, pointed out the difficulty of returning to life in society especially at such a young age and after a period of such brutality. "Many young men find great difficulty in returning to everyday life. Their lives are irreparably damaged."

Another large eagle stepped forward as the birds

gazed in awe at his fine plumage and strong, curved beak. "My name is Adnan," he said. "I am saddened by such stories, especially tales of children. These are truly stories of wasted youth. Often these accusations are not true, and even if they are true, stones thrown from a distance against huge armoured tanks are surely not lethal weapons. Sadly today this is one of the few activities available for children in a land where there is little to do because of the occupation."

One by one, the noble eagles stepped forward to tell their sad tales of humiliation and brutality. They also told stories of inspiring stories of Israeli women who visit the checkpoints to ensure that Palestinians are not being deprived of their basic rights. Other eagles brought forward stories of groups who try to stop the bulldozing of Palestinian houses. Palestinian and Israeli professionals – doctors, nurses, social workers and psychologists – also provided wonderful examples of how this tragic situation could be turned into something positive.

"We must now bring an inspiring tale from Ashkelon," said the Hoopoe bird.

The Wrath of Samson

"How much justice, goodness, and beauty can be created on earth if there is a decent will to it." Herzle M Altneulamn 1902

"The town of Ashkelon is near Gaza and in the Old Testament it is named as the place where thousands of years ago the mighty Samson was killed by his own hand. A prisoner in chains, he was taken to the temple of Dagon. His strength was such, that he was able to pull down the pillars, destroying the temple and killing himself and all the Philistines. Now Ashkelon is also the site of an infamous prison, housing both Palestinian and Israeli prisoners."

Rebecca a young, shy peacock stepped forward, her beautiful turquoise and olive-green tail, sweeping the soft ground. "A short time ago, Mordechai Vanunu was finally released from prison in Ashkelon; a hero for some, a traitor for others." Rebecca shook her head sadly: "I despair of any improvement in our world if we all view the same event so differently. This man was locked away in solitary confinement for nearly eighteen years because he did what his conscience told him to do – he explained to the world that Israel has nuclear weapons and has ignored many of the United Nations resolutions that regulate the use of nuclear material."

Rebecca shook her head from side to side, her voice becoming stronger as she developed the speech. "The world has gone to war in Iraq over a man who did not appear to honour UN resolutions on weapons of mass destruction. Now we know that there were in fact no weapons of mass destruction in Iraq. Indeed, since the invasion of Iraq, nuclear material has gone missing and may have fallen into the wrong hands. Yet few of the voices which condemned Saddam Hussein for his alleged possession of nuclear weapons have been heard to criticise Israel's nuclear capabilities. Indeed, the one brave Israeli who revealed Israel's nuclear secrets has been punished severely for his integrity and his honesty. What is happening to our world?"

All the birds murmured in agreement.

Another peacock, Nidal stepped forward, adjusted his sweeping feathers and began to continue the story:

— One Palestinian student Khaled, imprisoned during the first *Intifada* for throwing stones, told his story of being in the same prison as Mordechai Vanunu. Khaled had previously been in solitary confinement himself. Standing outside in the prison courtyard in all weathers, his hands were often tied behind his back and attached to a pipe running around the wall. His head was covered by a hood and if he asked to go to the bathroom he was badly beaten. Consequently, urine ran down his legs as he stood day after day for months in the scorching heat and freezing cold. This period of solitary confinement for Khaled lasted for six months; in the case of Vanunu it lasted nearly twelve years. In fact when he was told that he could spend the rest of his prison sentence with Israel prisoners he declined. He preferred instead to remain in his own cell, although by then he was allowed to walk in the corridor. In the jail, many of the Israeli prisoners regarded Vanunu as a traitor. They would accordingly insult him and victimise him at every opportunity. Khaled never understood how Vanunu in fact remained sane. —

The peacock stopped, pulling at his beautiful feathers as he quietly reflected on the situation: "Maybe he knew one day he would be vindicated by much of the world."

Simran sighed softly: "Vindicated, yes, and freed from prison but not yet free, not allowed to leave the country, not allowed to talk to foreigners. Is that justice for a stolen life?"

Daniel, a serious young owl, spoke up earnestly: "If being patriotic means not listening to our conscience, if love of our country means keeping quiet when we see injustice done, then that is very sad indeed."

There was silence for a while among the assembly of birds. Usually accustomed to thinking no more deeply than how to find food and survive in the wild, the birds were quite shocked to realise that the philosophical issues they were now being forced to confront were affecting them in a major way.

A sweet young peacock, Rachel, came down to the

podium, looked around shyly at all the birds, and hesitantly she began to speak:

"Some ordinary Israelis supported Vanunu as did many people from other countries who regarded him as a prisoner of conscience. However, apparently even Amnesty International did not know how to treat him for many years. This lack of support has always been a problem for individuals who declare themselves to be both pacifists and conscientious objectors. In the past, many governments and even church leaders and ordinary citizens have regarded pacifists as cowards and traitors. The political environment has changed a little in recent times but not yet enough to make this world a better and a safer place. Remember one thing – if soldiers refuse to fight, there will be no more wars.

When Vanunu himself was asked what kept him sane, he replied that he wished to leave prison still the same man he had been when he entered jail. They could take away his freedom but they could not break his spirit. Another, perhaps even more important point that he made was that he was able to remain sane because he knew he was doing the right thing. That is a very special reply and suggests to all of us that if we live our lives with integrity, we can endure all things."

At this Manga looked confused, and hopped from foot to foot impatiently trying to ask a question. "What exactly is integrity?" he asked at last, biting gently at his claw.

"It's not easy to explain in words," replied Rachel gently. "It is, however, easy to recognise when people are living with integrity. In the sense in which we are currently using the word, it is probably best defined as being true to yourself and living with values for the greater good – values with which you feel comfortable. Remember, Manga, doing something that makes you feel uncomfortable usually means that you are doing the wrong thing."

Manga scratched his head and tiny, brightly coloured feathers drifted to the ground. Dreamily he tried to catch them.

'I think I understand. Maybe it is similar to those times when you try to help another bird in distress. You may not want to do so because it could cause difficulties but you know you have no choice because it feels like the right thing to do."

Rachel smiled: "Mordechai Vanunu used many bird analogies when he described his stay in prison. He explained how, although he was under lock and key, he could set his spirit free like a bird and in his mind he could hover over places he loved, such as St. John's church in Sydney. Like a bird he could fly everywhere, re-creating memories and flying over places he had seen in the past. He saw himself as a caged bird who would keep his spirit free and one day fly again. He particularly enjoyed the beautiful sound of birdsong because he saw birds as symbols of peace and freedom, flying everywhere with no barriers and no boundaries. After several years in prison, doves came to his window, nesting and raising their young directly outside the cell where he was incarcerated."

Manga still looked puzzled, "Why did he do something which could have such awful repercussions?" he asked, picking at his feathers thoughtfully.

Rachel paused for a second, thinking of a man who had sacrificed so much. "Mordechai Vanunu studied philosophy at Be'er Sheva University. He was a pacifist and felt very strongly about the evils of war. Most of all however, he felt very strongly about the treatment of Palestinians by his own government."

The wise old owl Simsim sighed softly: "He is a very brave man, we can all learn a lot from his actions. The world must help to make him truly free and able to travel wherever in the world he wishes." The sound of chattering birds filled the air as together they tried for a while to find a solution to yet another tragic tale.

Bird after bird came forward and continued to tell their stories from all over Israel and Palestine – tales from both sides – accounts of Palastinians whose houses had been demolished, of Israelis who had tried to prevent those demolitions and to rebuild the damaged houses. Each bird was determined to contribute to the success of the conference in the hope that they too, in some small way, could help to make the world a better place.

Chapter 6

SHADOW OF FEAR

*"Mankind can be saved only if a supranational system,
based on law, is created to eliminate the methods of brute force"*
Albert Einstein

Next it was the turn of the birds of Jerusalem and in the distance the Golden Dome and ancient walls stood as silent witnesses to the importance of this city over the centuries. In an old church in Jordan is the oldest known map of Jerusalem. This mosaic map on the floor of the church in Madaba is dated fifth century AD. and depicts Jerusalem as the centre of the world. Many centuries later this ancient city still holds a special place in the hearts of many around the world.

Once again Hoopoe bird addressed the assembled group:

"This is a city central to the beliefs of the three great monotheistic religions with churches, mosques and synagogues battling for space within its ancient walls. Another battle is taking place outside its walls. While Israel has declared that Jerusalem is its eternal and undivided capital, the old City and East Jerusalem, Arab for generations, has been designated by the Palestinians as the capital of their future Palestinian State. The encircling Israeli settlements, and now the Wall, dividing and separating the Arab areas, are undermining these aspirations. Let us therefore hear a selection of stories from within this holy and historic city, spoken by birds of peace, those gentle Jerusalem doves."

The City of Solomon

"By non-violence, I do not mean passiveness, weakness, or surrender. Rather it is an empowerment and an ongoing struggle that requires inner strength and perseverance." Zoughbi Elias Zoughbi

Mustapha, a shy dove with soft brown eyes, stepped up to the podium ands began:

— Jerusalem is a city like no other in the whole world. It is a city of both astounding beauty and spiritual and cultural significance. I have built my nest among the mosaic patterned tiles under the Golden Dome. The Haram al-Sharif is one of the most beautiful structures in the holy city. Every day I look across at the Mount of Prayers where we now stand, and I listen to some of the voices of all faiths raised up to the heavens. The historical record states that the city was captured by King David some three thousand years ago and that his son Solomon built the First Temple there which was later destroyed by King Nebuchadnezzar of Babylon. The city changed hands again many times over the centuries. Those who left indelible marks in their wake include King Herod the Great, the Byzantines, the Crusaders and the Ottoman Turks. —

Mustapha looked sad as he thought about more recent times.

— Now it is a divided city under Israeli rule and also a city of great hardship and sadness. In villages around Jerusalem, stories abound of families whose houses have been bulldozed because they could not afford to buy a permit from the Israeli government to build on their own land. In the old city itself, Palestinians must ask for a permit in order to make improvements to their own houses. These permits often take a long time to be granted so although both these areas pay the same taxes, the Palestinian areas are in very bad condition whereas the Jewish areas are beautifully maintained. Many believe that the Israelis are doing this in the hope that the Palestinians will eventually abandon their houses, leaving Jerusalem to the Israelis. In some areas close to the Jewish quarter when the Palestinians leave their homes even for a couple of hours, their houses have been commandeered by Jewish families. As a consequence of this, there are Palestinian families who are now afraid to leave their houses empty at any time. Even when they have to attend weddings or funerals, they always leave at least one person behind to mind the house. —

"Sadly that is so," said Simran. "The Palestinian areas are in very bad condition because the municipality does not maintain them adequately, nor do they allow improvement of their own areas by the Palestinians themselves."

A tiny dove, Enjad, then stepped forward. Gently she started to speak:

— I have an inspiring story about a Palestinian village near Jerusalem where young boys and girls were helped to overcome adversity and achieve excellence against all odds. The main person in this story is a young boy Raad, whose aim was to go to Athens to swim in the Olympic Games. He trained in a chilly make-shift swimming pool built in connected gardens in less than a week by family and friends from the village. In the cold winter an attempt was made to conserve heat with sheets of nylon covering the pool under a corrugated roof. No one discloses the location of the pool because, although it is in a Palestinian village, the Israelis have not granted planning permission for the pool and it could therefore be demolished at any time. Many houses have in fact been bulldozed as a result of this inhumane policy.

In Raad's case, he studied at school all day and trained hard in his spare time. Unlike most other Olympic swimmers, he had no official sponsorship. His father, Hussein was badly in debt and could not afford to adequately heat the pool or pay for Raad's travel to international competitions. Despite all of this, Raad swam his laps with other students of all ages, six or seven swimmers in each lane. Many of these children were Palestinian champions. Among these children was one young boy whose father had been shot dead by Israeli soldiers. 'Hopefully,' said Hussein, 'this swimming pool is helping many young people to turn their frustration into constructive activity rather than violent behaviour.' By good fortune, Raad was brought to Europe by several foreign groups to participate in competitions and avail of modern training facilities. He managed in fact to represent Palestine at the 2004 Olympic Games in Athens, showing that by strength of character any adversity can be overcome. —

"That is an amazing story," said Benjamin enthusiastically, his slender head bobbing up and down. "Imagine the obstacles overcome by these young boys and girls who have to train in such difficult situations. It is also important that the world can see that despite all the difficulties, many Palestinians are trying to live normal and constructive lives."

"Jerusalem is also a place of great suffering because of the killing of innocent civilians in suicide bombings," added an older dove, Sami. "Killing must never be condoned. The only just way forward in any conflict is by dialogue. Sometimes this takes a long time but it is the only long-lasting solution. No progress has ever been made by the killing of innocent men, women and children on buses and in cafes. Israeli families have been torn apart with the only result being increased hatred on both sides and ever stronger calls for even more lethal retaliation. Collective punishment has been employed by the Israeli authorities as a supposed deterrent and many houses have been bulldozed in the West Bank and Gaza Strip leaving yet more innocent people homeless. These suicide bombings also give the world an excuse to ignore the injustices being perpetrated on the Palestinian people. Such inhuman actions could be seen as a form of war crime just as can the bombings of innocent civilians by governments, and both actions only play into the hands of those who want to see this tragic conflict continue."

"That is why I think that many of the truly brave people in the world are pacifists," mused Simran, the swallow softly.

"Simran, you always have to think differently from other birds," laughed Bassem tossing a tiny twig at the small swallow.

"Leave her alone, Bassem! The trouble with you is that you usually don't think at all!" Suha pushed the chubby sparrow and he fell over onto his back, his spindly legs in the air.

Simran was still turning the problem over in her mind. "I think it is important to be an independent thinker, not just to be different but to look at the world from all points of view and really work out what you feel is right. If you just follow the ideas of others you do not think about problems and that is a disaster."

"You are such a deep thinker, Simran," sighed Manga, full of admiration, "but why do you think that paficists are brave?"

"Pacifists!" Simran corrected Manga with a smile. "Because they are often misunderstood by the world which deems them cowards and traitors. True pacifists are not afraid to die but they do not want to be the cause of the death of others. The path of non-violence is the path we should try to follow and eventually we shall achieve our goals."

"That is exactly what has happened in Al Quds University," said Soraya excitedly, nodding her delicate head as she made her way to the platform to tell her story. "The President of the University, Sari Nusseibeh, who is a great advocate of non-violence, tried to stop the building of the Separation Wall through the campus. The University was going to be deprived of one third of its available land because of this Wall which was going right through the sports grounds. The President realised that he could not stop the Wall completely but he could at least try to move the path of the Wall and save some of the campus."

"Did he negotiate with the Israelis to try to achieve this?" asked Simran.

"Well, initially the Israelis would not talk and continued to build the Wall through the campus. Dr Nusseibeh therefore decided to delay the building by peaceful means. The students played basketball in the path of the Wall, they also played sports on other parts of the grounds and performed gymnastics in front of the men as they tried, unsuccessfully, to continue with their work of building the Wall. Meetings of journalists and foreign diplomats were held on the sports grounds and even university lectures and exams were held outside on the college grounds."

Soraya paused for a while as the birds reacted to her story enthusiastically. "Did it work?" asked Simsim, his owlish eyes huge and gleaming with excitement.

"Yes, it did work," answered Soraya. "All of this was carried out with good humour and as it is very difficult to continue building a concrete wall through smiling students who are playing games or listening to lectures, while the world press looks on, the Israelis were forced to negotiate and compromise and the Wall was pushed back a little so that less ground on the campus was confiscated."

"So the sports grounds were saved?" asked Omar.

"Fortunately, they were," said Soraya.

"The important point here, however, "said Hoopoe bird, "is that we learn that non-violence can work at least to some extent. If orchestrated correctly it is the most effective way to resolve conflict. Had violence or even violent words been used in this case, nothing would have been achieved and the University would have lost much of its land."

Hoopoe looked sad for a moment and then she composed herself as she continued. "We must also remember the many innocent people who have died in bombings in Jerusalem." The birds recalled harrowing scenes of bleeding bodies and burnt-out buses and cafes. Hoopoe called Talia the gentle Jerusalem dove to tell some sad tales.

Talia moved slowly to the podium, her dark eyes lowered as she remembered her distressing stories. "Many innocent Israeli and foreign students were killed and injured in the callous bombing in the café of the Hebrew University on the top of the beautiful Mount Scopus. It was a clear calm summer day and everything was so full of life and happiness and then the songs of the birds stopped and the air was filled with the sound of sirens as the spirit of death pervaded the top of the Mount."

"Why are people filled with such hate?" asked Rebecca the shy peacock, shuddering in horror. "Do they have no compassion for innocent people?"

"Well," said Talia softly, "often they have experienced tragedies of their own and they no longer feel for others as they try to gain revenge for themselves or for their nation. Sometimes they are young and impressionable and are used as pawns in a game played by others. As a nation the Palestinians have suffered so much and feel they have nothing else to lose. Eventually they must see, however, that nothing can excuse the killing of innocent people."

The birds murmured in agreement as Talia continued with her story.

"Another tragedy occurred in Jerusalem on the

intersection of Jaffa and King George street. That was a busy area and the bomber chose the Sbarro pizza restaurant filled with children and parents. Fifteen people died and over a hundred were injured as the huge bomb exploded destroying the restaurant and all the cars in the area."

The birds were very upset by these stories of lives ripped apart and wanted to know did any good ever come from such behaviour.

Talia shook her head. "Sadly, killings like these serve no purpose except to prolong suffering for everyone. They harden the response of the world and do no good whatsoever for the Palestinian cause. In fact these deeds just play into the hands of the evil people on both sides who do not want peace."

As Talia moved away from the podium, Hoopoe bird called for silence.

"There is one good aspect of this story," she said. "The organs of one Israeli victim of this atrocity were donated to the hospital, on his death, several weeks after the bombing. The next person on the list for a heart donation was a Palestinian man. When asked by the doctor, the widow of the Israeli man agreed that the Palestinian should receive the heart of her husband. That I think is a very special ending to such a terrible tragedy."

Hoopoe was getting tired and upset by all the stories and she uttered a loud sigh, "Now, let us bring tales from Gaza, a part of the country where much violence has taken place."

The Ancient Land of the Philistines

"In Palestine we are lost. We are without a homeland. It is stolen from us. Our very home has been stolen. Freedom is just a dream."
Yousef Shehada, Rafah refugee camp.

Hoopoe bird again began to speak: — Yousef is in a wheel chair; he is head of the Special Olympics movement in Palestine. He lives in Rafah refugee camp in the south of the Gaza Strip – one of the most densely populated places on earth and at present one of the most miserable. The Gaza Strip and the West Bank are predominantly Palestinian territories captured by Israel in the Six Day War. Historically, Gaza has always been an important Mediterranean town on the major trade routes linking Central Asia, Arabia and Persia with Europe and Egypt.

Now Gaza is a place of desolation. In certain areas, it is a barren landscape with mud roads destroyed and piles of rubble accumulating as more and more houses have been bulldozed. There is no sound of birdsong, little feeling of joy. Constant violence plagues Gaza. The Israeli army makes frequent incursions by tanks and planes into Gaza and Palestinian fighters fire missiles out of the camps into Israeli settlements and towns.

The people who suffer the most are the ordinary Palestinians who are killed and injured by Israeli raids, retaliatory or pre-emptive. There is little chance of employment and people are not allowed to enter or to leave without permits, including foreign aid workers.

Women suffer miscarriages, held up for hours at the notorious Erez checkpoint; sick people too wait there all day, trying to get to hospital and are often turned back. Children are shot and killed and people in wheelchairs are buried alive in their bulldozed houses and still the world keeps quiet. —

"Why is this?" asked Rebecca trying to make sense of a nonsensical situation.

"Perhaps because whenever the helicopter gunships make raids on Gaza they say they are targeting militants which always seems to justify their actions to the world. More often, however, they kill innocent civilians," said Hoopoe wearily, trying in vain to explain the inexplicable.

"Is there any difference between killing civilians in suicide bombings and killing innocent people in helicopter raids?" asked Rebecca again.

"Well," said Hoopoe, "both actions involve the death of innocent individuals, therefore, I can see no difference, except one act is carried out by so-called freedom-fighters and condemned by the world and the other is carried out with the tacit approval of world opinion, by a government who should know better."

"If that is so," said Rebecca, "to return to my original question, why does world opinion allow the Israeli government to kill innocent civilians when this same world is, quite rightly, horrified at suicide bombings?"

Hoopoe sighed softly, "I do not know," she admitted. "Perhaps the world is unaware of the true facts. The news always says that missiles were directed at militants. At this point the world stops listening. The fact that the 'militant' was in reality a man taking his pregnant wife to hospital in the middle of the night; a three year old child or a young boy who is running to help a wounded friend who is bleeding to death or a twelve year old schoolgirl carrying a school-bag full, not of bombs as reported but of books, does not make the headlines, at least not in the Western press. It does however get covered in Al Jezeera and other Arabic news channels which increases the risk of more attacks."

Gideon interrupted impatiently with a rush of words: "One time the army reported that the UN was loading weapons into ambulances. For weeks, this news was flashed around the world on television and in the press. Finally, it was admitted that this report had been incorrect, that the photo showed a stretcher not weapons. But this news was not reported on television or in the newspapers. In fact a member of the army had privately apologised to UN officials on the day after the original report, but no mention was made of this. Sadly, all kinds of ploys are used to discredit the UN." And he added, as an afterthought almost, "It seems that the truth doesn't matter."

Hoopoe appeared very desolate as she added: "It also appears that the world is afraid to challenge the one remaining superpower that is backing Israeli policy. If America changed its policy of unquestioning support for Israeli actions, this conflict could well be resolved much more effectively."

At this point Maha stepped forward anxious to enter the discussion: "It appears that a top aide to the Israeli government has claimed that the real aim of the 'Gaza disengagement plan' is in fact to prevent the formation of a Palestinian state. This plan to withdraw settlers from Gaza is intended to freeze the peace process while Jewish settlements can be even further enlarged on the West Bank. This has of course been formally denied but nevertheless West Bank settlements are continuing to expand contrary to international law."

"Gaza is indeed a tragic place." agreed Hoopoe bird with a sigh. "Let us hear some more. Let the seabirds of Gaza now step forward with their stories."

Omar, a large seagull moved shyly forward. "I would like to tell you more about Yousef Shehada," he said.

— 'A week of horror' is the way Yousef described what the Israelis termed *Operation Rainbow* in May 2004. 'The Rafah refugee camp was attacked at this time with the intention of finding tunnels. These hypothetical tunnels were alleged to be the means by which Palestinian resistance fighters brought in weapons through the Egyptian border although, after great destruction, nothing much was found.'

Yousef described how he lives close to this border, at what is enigmatically called the Philadelphi Route: 'We are used to Israeli shooting at our house and nearby houses, we are also used to the curfew that they impose every now and then but this time it was completely different. Tanks and helicopters went on shooting for twenty-four hours. They killed and destroyed everything they could reach. The destruction of people, houses, roads, trees and all infrastructure seemed to be the goal. Then our house and the whole area were surrounded by tanks and bulldozers. They did not like to use regular streets so their tanks passed through peoples' houses. Within two days they had destroyed thirty houses just around us. Most of the people were scared of the Israeli tanks, so they abandoned their houses. We were afraid so we stayed inside. Then the soldiers informed us that all the men should leave their houses. Again, we were afraid to leave so we stayed in hiding inside the house. Of those who did assemble outside, six men were killed." —

A white seagull, Maryam, swooped gracefully over the heads of the birds, her tail feathers in the shape of a delicate fan. Resting on the podium, she began to speak: "One poor woman from Gaza had to spend many months living in a tent with her two young daughters, in the terrible heat of summer," she said sadly.

"Her house was in the refugee camp in Rafah and it was bulldozed by Israeli tanks in May. All she had to eat for many weeks was bread and tomatoes. Her three-year old daughter suffered from glaucoma and could not see through her milky-white eyes. On many occasions she tried to take her daughter to hospital in Jerusalem but she was refused permission to leave Gaza. Despite this, whenever the woman was given anything, she immediately shared it with others."

Maryam paused. "I think we can learn a lot from the suffering of some of the people in Gaza. Another story which also gives me great sadness is about the zoo in Rafah. During this same incursion, Israeli tanks apparently destroyed much of the zoo's enclosures and many of the animals. Pictures showed beautiful parrots lying dead among the rubble and destruction. Apart from the killing of the animals, this also entailed the loss of a place of healing for the people of Gaza. Children and adults would come to the zoo to find a haven of peace in a land full of trauma."

The birds were silent again, once more quite shocked by what they had heard. The Hoopoe bird broke the silence. "There have been many deaths in Gaza over the last few years and we must remember several young foreigners who were killed within a few weeks of each other. One was American peace activist, Rachel Corrie, who tried to prevent houses being destroyed by standing in front of the bulldozers. She was confident that she could safely make a protest that would be dangerous for Palestinians. A young American girl, it was thought, would not be harmed in front of the world press. Some Israeli soldiers, however, appear to feel immune from all acts of destruction. Sadly, Rachel was crushed to death before the eyes of the world. Cameraman James Miller was shot from an Israeli tank while carrying a white flag and another peace volunteer Tom Hurndell was shot while trying to protect a young child. "

"Their names will live on," declared Einstein, with a sense of quiet determination. "Although sadly, the world does not hear about the many locals who were also killed."

"Indeed," said Hoopoe quietly, "we must make sure that if we cannot stop the killings of innocent people, then at least we can tell the world about these happenings."

Chapter 7

GARDEN OF PEACE

"You have rightly chosen," said God, "for in my
garden of Paradise this little bird shall sing for evermore,
and in my city of gold the Happy Prince shall praise me."
Oscar Wilde

The afternoon light was changing as a misty veil of cloud covered the blue sky. Hoopoe bird composed herself, shaking her black and white striped tail. With a clear voice she continued:

"We must leave Gaza for the moment," she said. "Let us move on to an inspiring story from Tel Aviv, the modern, cosmopolitan Israeli city. Our friends, the crow family, will tell us these tales."

The Hill of Springs

When the Tree rises up, the branches
shall flourish green and fresh in the sun
the laughter of the Tree shall leaf
beneath the sun
and birds shall return
Undoubtedly, the birds shall return.
The birds shall return.
Fadwa Toukan

Amal started with a description of Tel Aviv, a city only a century old that is situated on the beautiful

Mediterranean coast line. A modern city concerned more with finance and commerce than culture.

"I bring a story told by an academic and writer called Tami about a very special group of Israeli women," said Amal as she stepped up to the podium.

— Tami, herself, is a member of this group and speaks and writes about the concept of justice with great passion and eloquence. This group is called Machsom Watch and these women stand at the checkpoints to monitor violations of human rights. They started a few years ago at the Bethlehem checkpoint and at first their activities were quite sporadic. Now the group is more organised and there are two shifts daily at many checkpoints in the West Bank. One shift is in the morning when children go to school and people go to work, another is in the afternoon. —

Suha's eyes were shining as she heard this story. "That is a wonderful tale!" she exclaimed. "Can they really make a difference?"

"If all people were to behave with such integrity, there would be few difficulties in the world," added Hoopoe bird.

"When Machsom Watch began there were only twenty women standing at checkpoints, now there are four hundred. The Palestinian people are pleased to see the Israeli women there because they feel that by their presence some limits are being imposed on the actions of the soldiers. Their sense of being alone and powerless is also lessened. Now do you think that they make a difference?"

All the birds answered in unison, singing loudly in their sweet voices: "Yes, we do."

Amal smiled and continued with her account:

— The group writes reports and tries to make the soldiers accountable for their bad behaviour. There is a discussion at the moment, however, to decide the limits of Machsom Watch itself. Some women believe that they should just observe and report on the behaviour of soldiers and others think that they should intervene if they see a breach of human rights. Recently a Palestinian man was walking through a checkpoint when a woman soldier told him to open his jacket. When he did this she told him to open it a little more. The man was getting tired of the humiliation and told her 'Khalas' which means 'enough'. When this happened a male soldier again asked him to open the jacket still further and the man pushed him aside. One of the Israeli women who was standing at the checkpoint ran forward when she saw this, in order to stand between the man and the soldiers. Another soldier pushed her to the ground and started to kick her. He then pulled her up by the neck and wrapping his fingers around her throat, he tried to choke her with his two thumbs. —

The birds gasped in horror at this. "Can you imagine what they do to Palestinians at these checkpoints, when they are capable of abusing an Israeli woman in this way?" asked Einstein grimly, as he shook his bright-red tail feathers vigorously.

"Yes, indeed I can," said Amal nodding her head sadly. "So too can these brave women in Machsom Watch, which is why they continue to commit themselves to this thankless task."

One by one the crows stepped forward with their tales, strong intelligent birds with charcoal grey bodies, black-capped heads and shiny black wings.

"We must also remember the innocent victims of senseless violence," added Nazih, a thoughtful crow who always looked at situations from every point of view. "Bars and cafes have been destroyed by bombs in this city and many buses have been blown apart. There are no winners in these situations. Killing can never be excused."

The birds were greatly distressed by this talk of loss of innocent lives. "Maybe," said Simran thoughtfully "we should tell more stories of innocent children killed in restaurants and buses, maybe we should try to be more balanced." The birds nodded their heads in agreement as they thought of the many atrocities committed in Tel Aviv.

Hoopoe once again started to speak: "As many great Israeli journalists have suggested, it is important to be fair but it is difficult to be balanced in this conflict. How can we be balanced when one side has nuclear and other weapons of mass destruction and the might and finance of a superpower behind it. How can we be balanced when so many more innocent Palestinians die than do innocent Israelis. No one knows about these deaths which occur everyday, whereas the whole world screams in indignation, and rightly so, when there is a bombing against the Israelis. The purpose of our conference is to tell the world tales it seems to know nothing about. One famous Israeli journalist says that his writings about what happens under the occupation are destined for the archives. This is so that in future years, no-one can say they were not told what was going on."

As the light began to fade, the birds were tiring but still they continued to approach the podium with their stories. Hoopoe bird began to introduce the owls bringing stories from the ancient West Bank town of Hebron.

The City of Abraham

"Oppressors will always deny that they are oppressors. All I can do is bear witness and set down what I saw and heard and what the strange journey of my life has been. Suffering is written now in the valleys and mountains of Tibet." Palden Gyatso

"Inside the Ibrahimi Mosque in the centre of the old city of Hebron is the presumed burial place of Abraham, Isaac, Jacob and their wives. This site is accordingly of great importance to both Jews and Muslims. Several years ago, a Jewish settler named Baruch Goldstein who was originally from New York opened fire and killed many Muslims at prayer in the mosque, so there is now much more security. Hebron was a thriving business town with a lovely old souq with vaulted ceilings and tiny shops selling, among other things, the hand-blown glass for which Hebron is famous. Now there are no tourists to buy the delicate pastel-coloured glasses and bowls. The old city is dead. Settlers have moved in and attack the townspeople on a daily basis. There is a lot of trouble in Hebron especially with regard to the surrounding settlement Qiryat Arba which is right on the edge of Hebron. Life is full of sadness in a once thriving town. Now, my wise friends the owls, please step forward to read or tell your stories."

Simsim, the wise old owl, stepped forward first to tell his tale:

— Little stalls are dotted along the settler road outside Hebron. These stalls are overflowing with colourful grapes, figs, plums, peaches and apples as Palestinians try to sell their produce. One day, two foreign women stopped to buy fruit at the roadside. Seeing two Israeli tanks speeding down on the other side of the road they asked the owner of the shop what was happening. The man answered that the Israeli soldiers frequently came to overturn the stalls and throw the fruit down the valley. He told the women that the Israelis claim it is dangerous for people to stop to buy the fruit. Palestinians, however, are desperate to sell their produce which is often their only means of earning a living. They have no option, therefore, but to continue risking the anger of the Israelis.

The foreigners turned their car and followed the jeep which had by then stopped at a stall a short distance down the road. Two soldiers remained in the jeep and two others began harassing a group of old Palestinian women and young children. The foreign women demanded the names of the soldiers and threatened to report them if they continued their intimidation of the local people. At this, the driver called the two soldiers back into the jeep while the women discussed what was happening. After five minutes the jeep drove away, leaving the fruit safe for that day, at least. The old Palestinian women explained that this was a regular occurrence and their fruit was often tipped over into the nearby Wadi al Sheikh. —

"I think," said Simsim, softly, "the Israeli policy is not only killing the Palestinian people, they are also killing the Palestinian economy." Simsim then returned to his old perch on the branch of an ancient grey-green olive tree and watched proudly as the younger owls stepped forward.

"That is a very good point," said Samuel, a young, earnest owl. "Maybe it is not official policy but unfortunately whatever policy, it is working to the detriment of the Palestinians, who cannot get a decent market price for their fruit. The prices they get are now so low that the money they earn from the sale is less than the amount it costs to transport the produce. Consequently grapes are left on the vines to rot, you can see this all over Hebron. One local man found that he could not sell his grapes – he had more than twenty tons – a week later he suffered a fatal heart attack."

"That is tragic," said Taissir with feeling; "the poor man can only have died of a broken heart."

A strong, young owl Fadi stepped up to the podium, "I bring a story that must be told," he shouted with great passion as he began to read from the scroll he held in his claws. "International and Israeli peace activists and human rights lawyers want the world to know this story. It is a story about harassment and violence from Israeli settlers perpetrated on villagers in the thousand year old Southern West Bank village of Al-Tuwani. In the neighbourhood some villagers live in ancient caves carved out of the rock. Children are attacked on the way to school, as are foreigners who accompany them."

Maryam beat the air with her wings. "That happened in Northern Ireland, I think," she said hesitantly. "Young children on the way to their primary school were harassed and attacked by adult neighbours who thought that the children were threatening their way of life."

"Indeed," said Hoopoe. "There are many similarities between conflicts in so many countries. The situation, however, starts to improve when people begin to talk and negotiate, just as is happening in Northern Ireland. Fadi please continue."

"The only clinic that serves the area is in Yatta which is thirty minutes away from Al-Tuwani by car. Since the Israeli military regularly destroys the only road that leads there, the villagers have to go a long and difficult way to Yatta by donkey or tractor. Al-Tuwani began building its own clinic but Israeli authorities have repeatedly interfered with the construction. During the seasons of planting and harvesting, settlers frequently attack Palestinian farmers. The village has electricity for only four hours at night. It has one well which is fed from a spring and this provides water for drinking and cooking but does not provide enough water for washing. Rainwater is collected for animals and washing purposes. The villagers fear that if their story is not told, the expansion of Israeli settlements and settler violence will threaten their very existence. One inspiring Israeli, Ezra, works tirelessly to help villagers and to spread the word of their plight. He is constantly arrested and harassed by certain soldiers who resent his presence in the area. The villagers have nothing and Ezra collects money, toys and clothes to help them survive."

"Survival is almost impossible in the South Hebron Hills," said Soraya, "especially now that projections show that Al-Tuwani is going to be on the Israeli side of the Wall."

"I bring another sad story," said a young owl called Noor, fluffing out her soft feathers.

— One family in Beit Omar, a village on the edge of Hebron told us their story about their son Amjed, a twenty-two year old who had studied journalism and photography at Hebron university.. The people in the village heard the soldiers saying that on the following day they would kill two young boys in order to teach the village a lesson. Apparently some boys had been throwing stones at the tanks and the soldiers were very angry. The next evening Amjed Bahjet Alami was locking up his photography shop with his younger brother, when he heard the Israeli Defence Forces on the road. Frightened, the two brothers hid behind a wall. After a while they peeped out and Amjed was hit in the head. His younger brother carried his dying body back home. The roads were blocked off and no ambulance could get in to try to help him. The next day at the funeral, Amjed's cousin was also shot dead. Seven months later, Amjed's brothers were put in prison in the Negev, one for six months and one for two years. The charge was that they had been throwing stones at the funeral. Almost every day there is constant provocation from the army in Beit Omar. The soldiers drive by the mosque and start to shoot. Young children then chase the tanks and jeeps. The soldiers jump out of their vehicles, hide behind them and shoot at the children. —

Noor stopped, breathlessly and looked around at the group of birds for a reaction. The birds, however, had heard too much and were transfixed with horror, unable to respond to yet another tragic tale of wasted young life. Unsure what to do, Noor decided to continue with one final story.

— This same family pointed out a pile of rubble, the remains of a small house demolished by the Israelis because it was too close to the settler road. This house had been built by the community for a man who was paralysed nine years ago when a truck crushed him at his workplace. He spent a year in hospital and then friends and community joined together to help him. A pile of stones is all that is now left of his home. —

Manga hid his tiny head under his wing. "I cannot take any more cruelty; the pain on both sides is too hard to bear."

"Permits which Palestinians have to buy in order to build houses have written on them 'living but not owner'. But it is Palestinian land," shouted Suha puffing out her nut brown feathers in anger.

"I know, "said Simsim resignedly picking at his feathers, "but the world does not seem to want to hear the facts."

Hoopoe bird stood quietly at the podium as she watched their distress. She realised that the birds were tired and the stories were taking their toll. They needed to hear some healing words of comfort to get them through the long night.

"Maybe we should bring this conference to a close by telling a last inspiring story about the pursuit of excellence," she said softly. "About when the Israelis closed down the university in Hebron for six months. The students continued to study and the teachers continued to teach. They met each other anywhere they could – in bus stations and in cafes. Lessons were held in any rooms or houses which were available. Many students in other countries take their education for granted. In Palestine education is valued because life is so difficult."

Hoopoe had been deeply moved by all the tales of suffering and realised that, in order to help heal the spirits of the birds, she first needed to summon a state of calm within her own anguished soul. Standing alone in deep contemplation, she touched a centre of inner calm within herself. Regaining her strength she was then able to give the birds her blessing for a peaceful night.

"May the peace of ages rest on you this night and may your souls soar with angels so that you wake refreshed, able to continue with hope along the difficult path that lies before you."

It was growing cool now as the evening breeze scattered the last sun-ripened olives of autumn onto the winding paths. The olives glistened like shiny black tears spilling over the coral-tinted stones. Overhead wisps of white clouds swirled across the vaulted, violet sky like a never-ending kaleidoscope. The sleepy birds settled down to rest, sheltered among the comforting boughs of the towering cypress trees. Peace rested lightly on the Mount of Olives and sleep hung gently on the night air. The birds were drowsy and only the wind seemed to be awake as it whispered softly its secret messages. Lost in their own dreams, no one appeared to see or hear a small brightly coloured parrot leaving silently under a misty veil of darkness.

Chapter 8

THE SPREADING OF THE WORD

He will wield authority over the nations and
adjudicate between many peoples; these will hammer
their swords into ploughshares, their spears into sickles.
Nation will not lift sword against nation,
there shall be no more training for war.
Isaiah 2: 3–4

As another day broke, the charcoal-grey Mountains of Moab were transformed into an artist's palette of mauves and pinks. The dazzling rays of the sun painted the dusty Jordanian hills and breathed life into the pale blue hue of the Dead Sea, just as it had since the time of Moses. Ribbons of light and shade traced a path across the Mount of Olives as the sun rose over the ancient city of Jerusalem. The early morning sunlight gently brushed the gilded Dome on the Rock and the silence was broken by the call of the *muezzin* from the mosques echoing across the valley. Birds were stirring and awakening, full of hope on this the final day of the Conference.

Hoopoe bird stood behind the podium and waited patiently as the owl chorus assembled. Rustling their grey feathers and rubbing their sleepy eyes, they adjusted their tiny spectacles and prepared to copy down their final words. Hoopoe looked across at Omar and hesitated as she became aware of the absence of Manga. Always a favourite with all the birds, the tiny parrot was usually perched on the outspread wings of the large sea bird, holding on tightly with his claws. Now Omar was sitting alone, puzzled as he looked around for his colourful companion.

The other birds chattered anxiously too, worried about the fate of the much-loved parrot. Suddenly the peace was shattered as a small bird tumbled out of the sky and skidded to an abrupt halt at the foot of the podium. An excited cry resounded through the group, "Manga is back!"

In his beak Manga carried a tiny olive branch. He spoke quietly to Hoopoe and then turned to face the assembly of birds:

"I have returned from Ramallah bearing sad news – the leader and inspiration of the Palestinian nation, Yasser Arafat, is dead."

Manga gently laid the grey-green olive branch on the podium and again addressed the birds: "I bring back an olive branch in memory of the visit of President Arafat to the United Nations thirty years ago when he carried an olive branch in one hand and a gun in the other, asking that he should not be forced to lay down the olive branch.

Sadly this legendary figure has now passed away. Last night I heard the news which was told to me by the secret voice of the night wind and I set off immediately for Ramallah. Yasser Arafat died in Paris and his funeral will take place in the grounds of the Muqata today, the last Friday of Ramadan. People are already gathering there in their thousands to pay their respects."

Manga paused at this point as the shocked birds talked together in reverent, hushed tones: "This is not just the death of a person but the death of a symbol of statehood. A leader of a state which was promised but was not to come to pass in his lifetime," continued Manga. "He was by no means perfect, like all human beings he made errors but his vision for his people and his country cannot be denied. Because of him, the world at last pays attention to the problems of a nation without a state. Let us now pray that like the mythical Phoenix rising from the ashes of its own death, a new Palestine can arise from the ashes of its dead leader."

All the birds were deeply upset by this news and began to speak quietly among themselves. The Hoopoe bird quickly called for silence. As she began to speak, she seemed a distant, regal figure with her head held high and her royal crest standing erect along the top of her head. She stood there quietly, her black and white striped wings folded back as her tail lay draped at her feet, like a royal train.

"O Allah, may the leader of the nation of Palestine finally attain in death the peace and freedom which he has been denied in life and may the Palestinian and Israeli people also grow and flourish in peace and justice."

The birds bowed their heads, lost in thought. With tears in her eyes, Hoopoe bade farewell to the other birds. "My good friends, my task here is now finished. My journey will soon be over as I cast off this earthly shell and go through the valley of death to unite with the Sacred Bird – the Simurgh."

There was an atmosphere of great sadness as the birds listened to her words. They all felt confused and alone without the guidance of this wise and knowing bird who had always so freely given so much of herself.

"Go with my blessing to follow in the footsteps of the prophets Moses and Mohammed and to walk in the shadow of Christ who many years ago in this Holy City asked his disciples to spread the Word. Today may the finger of Allah point your Way in the sky as you fly over snow-tipped mountains and ice-blue seas and may He trace your Path in the grains of sand as you traverse the burning deserts. May you be guided by the golden light of the sun and by the silver light of the moon and guarded by angels as God holds you gently in the palm of his hand. This day I ask you to spread the Word so that all peoples can live in peace together in this Holy Land."

The birds remained silent, as they listened to the final words of Hoopoe bird.

Then one by one the owl chorus rolled up their manuscripts and neatly tied them with ivy twine. They presented the scrolls with a solemn bow to The Hoopoe bird. Returning their dignified bow, she silently handed one manuscript to each of the five birds who stepped forward with great pride and who were also filled with a deep sense of humility: Einstein, Suha, Omar, Simran and Manga. Bowing deeply once again, Hoopoe then took the final manuscript in her beak.

At this sign the thousands of birds rose like a multi-coloured tapestry into the air and flew in the direction of the town of Bethlehem. This magic carpet swooped rhythmically across the Kidron Valley, the Valley of Jehoshaphat as it is known in the Old Testament. Devout Jews believe it is here that the bodies of the dead will be resurrected on the Day of Judgment.

Moving in unison, the birds passed over the gracious buildings of Government House on the Hill of Evil Counsel. They flew over the Israeli settlement of Har Homa and over the armed soldiers standing at the checkpoints. They passed over the Separation Wall and across the site of Rachel's Tomb. People were amazed and pointed upwards as the strange cloud of birds darkened the sky and blotted out the sun.

Finally the birds assembled over the ancient biblical town of Bethlehem, forming a vast star shaped shadow centered over the Church of the Nativity and Manger Square. These thousands of birds were determined to carry their messages of peace to the entire world. In the middle of this star formation were five birds, each holding a rolled scroll and each one ready to carry out a special task. Four of these birds were entrusted to take a manuscript to each corner of the earth. The task of the fifth bird, Manga, was to bring a scroll to Israel to explain to those who did not know what was happening in their land and in their names.

For a few minutes the birds rested over Bethlehem, the beautiful old stone buildings glowing rose-pink in the late afternoon light. Then the points of the star began to elongate and thin out as the birds commenced their journeys to all the peoples of the world.

Many of these birds knew that they would never return. They set off nevertheless with a sense of great hope, to ride on the wind and clouds, to whisper to the flowers and to enter the dreams of people everywhere in order to spread the word and tell the world the truthful stories it did not seem to want to hear. The suffering of these birds would be great but because this suffering was for a purpose, it could and would be endured.

A few miles away, the Garden of Gethsemane was enveloped by a heavy velvet mist. Hoopoe watched the final birds start on their long journeys as the Jerusalem sky darkened and the sun set into the Mediterranean Sea. Gently digging with her slender curved beak among the pink and purple cyclamen, she placed the final manuscript in the soil under one of the ancient olive trees where it would remain as a testament for future generations.

Hoopoe shivered slightly as the night closed in around her and she felt the first icy touch of winter. Raising her curved beak to the heavens, she uttered this prayer:

> "Attar, you who have travelled through the valley of death, lead these birds in your footsteps. May this journey end in hope and in the rebirth of the world to peace and to justice."

EPILOGUE

"At what point will you say no to this war?
We have chosen to say, with the gift of liberty, if necessary, our lives:
The violence stops here, the death stops here, the suppression of the truth
stops here, the war stops here. Redeem the times!"

Fr. Daniel Berrigan

Suspended in the stillness of time, the silver moon slides slowly out of view behind the charcoal smudge of the headland. At the mouth of the bay, the light house stands like a lone sentinel, the harsh flash of its rays of light piercing this darkest hour of the night. Seated on a rock holding the weathered manuscript scroll in my hands, I gaze out to sea. My mind is still absorbing those terrible stories from that far-off land.

So much has happened since that conference of birds took place and, sadly, peace is as elusive as ever. The scapegoat is dead but a new one has been found. Disengagement has occurred in Gaza from where Omar had travelled to report his stories, but the peace process is no more. Gaza has descended further into chaos: people are starving, its economy has collapsed. Gaza is an open prison, borders blocked and seas patrolled. Through the summer just past, artillery shells rained down on the burnt-out land. I had watched this as the world said nothing. Gaza is now dying.

In the West bank, the Wall, which so angered Ali and the other quails from Jayyous, continues to stride across the land like a massive millipede, its footprints crushing everything in its path, tearing through olive groves and destroying livelihoods. The illegal settlements grow larger as roads and towns spill out across the land, leaving no room for a viable Palestinian state. The Jerusalem envelope is almost sealed. This Wall swoops and loops around huge illegal settlements drafting them into the Holy City. But the Palestinian villages formerly in Jerusalem are now excluded.

Things have happened that Hoopoe bird and her colleagues couldn't have foreseen at their conference. The free nations of the West, for instance, have now cut off money from the democratically elected Palestinian Authority. As a result it cannot pay the salaries of teachers, policemen and other members of the public service essential to its survival. Democracy spoke and those who voted are being collectively punished for their choice. Everyone knows that is not justice; that is not a way forward to peace.

Across from the Golan Heights, the Land of the Cedars is destroyed. Cities and villages are razed to the ground and, again, the world sits back and waits ...

My mind struggles too with the distorting lens of language in the mouths of the powerful: words and phrases circling for dominance, leaving me wearied and helpless to determine even my own understanding. What might Hoopoe bird have said in the simplicity of her birdspeak about the use and misuse of words to distract and confuse: words such as – 'balance', 'martyr', 'disproportionate', 'sacrifice', 'anti-Semitism', 'state-violence', 'terrorist', 'good', and 'evil'.

It is with a heavy heart that I begin to roll up the manuscript. Wine-red juice is spreading across its text, words blurring in the lightly-falling autumn rain. As I clamber up the granite steps, daylight breaks and seabirds begin to gather.

The task that Hoopoe gave to the birds of the air in Israel and Palestine is done. They braved the heat and the freezing cold; they flew over burning sands and icy mountaintops; they told their stories. Many will have since died of exhaustion; for some, their time will have come; few will return to their Sacred Land.

I know now why the seagull braved the distances between us to drop this scroll at my feet. The task has been passed on to those of us who care, and who know of the story; to all who have listened to these tales, and to all who will read the scroll. For the silence of the world shames each of us, makes us complicit, and turns this conflict into our conflict too. What has been left to us is the breaking of that silence, and also the hopes and blessings of the Hoopoe bird …

The End

THE SONG OF THE BIRD

by Rima Nasir Tarazi

O lucky, happy bird!
O lucky, happy bird!
You are so free and blithe
While I'm oppressed and sad.
O lucky, happy bird!
Please save me little bird!

At midnight they broke in
My father they detained
They beat and tortured him
Then exiled him enchained.
O lucky, happy bird!
Please save me little bird!

They bombed grandfather's house
And bulldozed every stone;
Our people they dispersed
And drove away from home.
O lucky, happy bird!
Please save me little bird!

My valiant brother fought
With rocks and burning tires:
Courageously he sought
To save his home and brothers.
O lucky, happy bird!
Please save me little bird!

Go tell ye little bird!
Go tell in all the world
Tell everyone concerned
What you have seen and heard.
Please save me dear bird!

O teach me to be free
To live in dignity;
And teach me how to sing
While they their bullets fling
O teach me little bird!
Please save me dear bird!

Dedicated to Palestinian children on the occasion of the International Year of the Child, 1979. This song was first performed by the children of the Society of In'ash El Usra in El Bireh at the YWCA in Jerusalem in 1979.

By Rima Nasir Tarazi (from her CD Ila Mata (Until When) Songs from Palestine, *sung by soprano Tania Nasir Tarazi. (ESNCM's website: www.birzeit.edu/music). She says of the origins of this song: "Soon every Palestinian home was to be touched by the brutality of the occupation. This led to a need to record my emotions in my own words and music .... The first such song was 'The Song of the Bird', which I wrote for the children of the Society of Inash el Usra."*

INFORMATION NOTES & REFERENCES

CHAPTER 1

Page 11: Conference of the Birds. A twelfth-century allegorical Persian work by Sufi philosopher, Farid ud-Din Attar

Page 12: The hoopoe bird, known as the *hud-hud* in Arabic because of the sound it makes, is regarded as a sacred messenger bird of good fortune

Page 13: Intifada is the Arabic word for 'uprising' or 'rebellion'.

Page 14: In the days of the British Mandate (1920–1948) militant groups from both the Jewish and Arab population who engaged in acts of terror were known as freedom fighters.

Page 15: Arabic for 'God is Great'.

CHAPTER 2

Page 25: Besserman, Pearl, ed, *The Way of the Jewish Mystics*, Boston: Shambala, 1994

Page 25: Simurgh in Persian means 'thirty birds'.

Page 30: See Frankl, Victor, *Man's Search for Meaning*, New York: Simon and Schuster, 1984

Page 31: Hijab is the generic term for the Islamic head covering for women.

CHAPTER 3

Page 37: The Dalai Lama, *The Little Book of Wisdom*, London: Rider, 1997

Page 39: Raheb, Mitri, *Bethlehem Besieged*, Minneapolis: Fortress Press, 2004

Page 41: Story told by Zoughbi Zoughbi, director of Wi'am (Conflict Resolution), Bethlehem

Page 44: Story told by Nasser Lehem

CHAPTER 4

Page 51: Chomsky, Noam, *Fateful Triangle – The United States, Israel and the Palestinians*. (Pluto Press, London, 1999)

Page 52: The Third Way, A Journal of Life in the West Bank by Raja Shehada. Quartet Books, London, 1982.

Page 53: A dunum is equivalent to approximately one quarter acre

Page 58: Said, Edward W, *After the Last Sky – Palestinian Lives*. London: Faber and Faber, 1996

Page 60: MEND, Middle East Non-Violence and Democratisation, a Palestinian NGO based in East Jerusalem

Page 63: In *Poetry Ireland Review*. Ed M. Smith, 2002/03, Issue 75. 'A House' by Palestinian poet and novelist, Zakaria Mohammed, b. Nablus 1951.

CHAPTER 5

Page 69: 'Thanks be to God' – a universally used Arabic expression.

Page 70: Statement made by dissident group of Israeli soldiers (2003).

Page 71: for a detailed discussion of child prisoners, see *Stolen Youth: The Politics of Israel's Detention of Palestinian Children.* Catherine Cook, Adam Hanieh and Adah Kay. Pluto Press, London, 2004.

Page 74: Among the many groups undertaking excellent work are Machsom Watch, Physicians for Human Rights, Women in Black, the Israeli Committee against House Demolitions, B'tselem and Parents' Forum: Bereaved Parents for Peace.

Page 75: From Eban, Abba, *My People, The Story of the Jews*, Weidenfeld & Nicolson: London 1969.

CHAPTER 6

Page 81: Subtle is the Lord: The science and the Life of Albert Einstein by Abraham Pais. Oxford University Press, Oxford, 1982.

Page 82: Zoughbi, Zoughbi Elias, *Faith and the Intifada*, Naim S Ateek, Marc H Ellis, Rosemary Radford Ruether ed, New York: Orbis Books, 1992

Page 85: Army of Roses: Inside the World of Palestinian Women Suicide Bombers by Victor, Barbara. Emmaus, Pennsylvania, USA: Rodale Press, 2003.

Page 95: The so-called Philadelphi Route comprises a large solid metal barrier some 25 feet high running along much of the border between the Gaza Strip and Egypt. Alongside the barrier Israel has demolished all dwelling houses and other buildings for a distance of about 200 metres to create a 'free-fire zone' which is now utterly bare and desolate.

Page 96: the destruction of the Rafah Zoo was reported on by Nuala Haughey in *The Irish Times*

CHAPTER 7

Page 99: Wilde, Oscar, *The Happy Prince*.

Page 99: poem by Fadwa Toukan (d. 2003, aged 86), known as the *Poet of Palestine*. Born in Nablus, she had no formal education in her youth but has published eight poetry collections, which were translated into many languages.

Page 103: Gideon Levy, journalist, *Ha 'aretz*.

Page 103: Gyatso, Palden, *Fire under the Snow, Testimony of a Tibetan Prisoner*, The Harvell Press, Great Britain, 1997

Page 106: Holy Cross school in Ardoyne, north Belfast

Page 109: So-called 'settler roads' have been built by the Israeli authorities to by-pass Palestinian towns and villages in the West Bank. Palestinians require permits to travel on them and are forbidden to build houses within a specified distance of them.

CHAPTER 8

Page 117: Government House was constructed in the 1930s to serve as an official residence for the British High Commissioner in Palestine. It is currently the headquarters of the United Nations Truce Supervision Organisation which was established to monitor the terms of the 1949 Armistice between Israel and the Arab States.

EPILOGUE

Page 123: 'Breaking the Silence' is the name of a group of soldiers from the Israeli Defence Forces who speak out about their actions in the occupied Palestinian territories.

"Action is the life of all and if thou dost not act, thou dost nothing."
Gerrard Winstanley

"The power of storytelling in the face of tragedy gives us reason to hope ..."
Seamus Cashman